CALLED UP
A LACROSSE STORY

DON MCDUFFEE

This book is dedicated to the memory of my father who passed away on July 7th, 2010. Dad, your daily displays of courage and strength will inspire all that knew you. You are missed and loved enormously. This book is also dedicated to those that have cancer or are fighting it. My heart goes out to the families that have lost a loved one to this horrible disease. My wife, Patty and my mother are both breast cancer survivors. They both battled cancer quietly and heroically. I can not begin to put into words how much I love them and how grateful I am that they are both with us today. Unfortunately, cancer is all too common and we all have friends and family members that have been affected by this disease. No less than ten percent of the profits from this book will be donated to research or charities that combat this disease. The book is also dedicated to all those playing, coaching or supporting lacrosse. Lacrosse: live it and love it from the cradle to the grave. It will always give you more than you give it.

ACKNOWLEDGMENTS

A special thanks goes out to those that made this book possible. Without their diligent work and support this book would not have become a reality. This group includes Maggie Kiernan, Colleen Krause and Tom Caputo. My wife Patty and to the kids that I have coached through the years.

FOREWORD

I had the good fortune of growing up in Massapequa, NY and I was equally lucky to have great neighbors. My name is Don McDuffee and coincidently I lived across the street from the Duffy's. At the time, the Duffy's had what must've been the only lacrosse goal in town in their backyard. The two Duffy brothers, John and Mike, were always in the backyard dodging and shooting on the goal. They would often be joined by their friends: Craig Jaeger, two sets of brothers, the Marino's (Billy and Tom) and the O'Neil's (Jake and Mike), and a few other friends. Those of you that recognize these names know the spectacular skills that my neighbors and I saw on display; therefore, you also know why we immediately fell in love with the game of lacrosse.

A few years later, I would go on to see several of these guys in the epic NCAA championship game at Rutgers. Mike O'Neil and the Johns Hopkins Blue Jays snapped the Marino's, Craig Jaeger, Eamon McEneaney and the Cornell Big Red's 42 game winning streak. It was a huge thrill for my Massapequa Mohawk team and me to attend the game. As I think back to my introduction to lacrosse, I can still hear the Duffy's dog, Bandit, barking like crazy as he wanted to join the game, and the tune Little Willie Wonk blasting on the radio; these were great times and I've loved the game ever since.

I played my youth lacrosse at John J. Burns Park for the Massapequa Mohawks. We were coached by two very dedicated men, Ed Harney and Warren O'Neil. On many occasions, John Kirby from the Massapequa High School team would come to help out. They drilled us constantly on fundamentals and unselfish play. Today John is a good friend and our sons play with and against each other in tournaments, and they too are friends. I remember our Mohawks team as if it was yesterday. On attack we had Ed Harney (UVA), John "Earl" Campbell (C.W. Post) and Scott Campbell (Special Forces), no relation to Earl. Our midfield consisted of my best friend on the team, Jerry O'Brien (Towson), Tim Mulligan (Cornell), Bruce Chanenchuk (Hopkins), Bobby Cummings (Cornell), Mike Seckler (wrestled at Penn State) and me (Loyola). On defense we had Ed Iannone (Navy), Pat Mulcahy (Post), Steve Ferrara and our goalies Pat Nugent and Kenny O'Neil. Our coaches taught us the game and we simply loved playing and being together before, during, and after practices and games.

My son and daughters now play in the Town of Oyster Bay Lacrosse League and all of their games are played at John J. Burns and a new field, the Field of Dreams. John J. Burns was always a great park, but it has been tremendously improved and is maintained beautifully. The most significant upgrade is the addition of field turf; my kids don't play in the same goose crap that I did. Currently, my family and I live in Huntington which is a half hour from the fields, but I never mind the trip down to Pequa, as I always get to see some old friends and my kids enjoy the same All American burgers and legendary fries that I loved as a kid.

My parents' home is still in Massapequa and they would make just about every game that my kids played down there, that's about 20 to 25 a year. My father passed away this last July and I am grateful that my kids played in the Town of Oyster Bay League because I was able to see my dad at least 50 to 100 times more than I would have over the last couple of years of his life. My father was one of the last polio victims in the United States and had very severe arthritis due to post-polio syndrome. I would call to tell my mother about games and she would often tell me that she didn't see how it would be possible for my father to make it, but come face off time he would be there—taking handicap parking to new heights, driving over curbs and sidewalks to pull his car right up to the fence for the best view of his grandkid's (Regan, Kara and Caitlyn) games. Dad, I love you and miss you.

I followed in my father's footsteps and attended Chaminade High School in Mineola. I was once again very lucky to have the lacrosse gods smile on me as I was coached by two legends of the game—Coach Robert Pomponio and Coach Jack Moran. These two men have been teaching and coaching at Chaminade for over 30 years and they have sent players to just about any school you can think of. They are great coaches, mentors and men. My team and I were also coached by some colorful guys named Jay Runac, John Espey and Artie Secamp; they too were definitely excellent coaches and fun to play for. At Chaminade I would also make tremendous friends with my equally colorful teammates. Guys like Vinnie Connors, Billy Golden, John Layden, Gerry Byrne, Ripper, Skull Bones, Joe DiOrio, the Pujols brothers, Pete Pace, Joe Coffey, Kevin Doyle, Tony Staltare, Tommy Hunter, John Orphanos, John Elarde and the sophs Tim McDevitt and Dave Kotowski.

Toward the end of my time at Chaminade, I was all set to attend Rochester Institute of Technology. Coach Moran had me setup to play for Bill Tierney up there, who had just been named the DIII Coach of the Year. Meanwhile, my mom had attended Mount St. Agnes College, an all girl's school that merged with Loyola College in Maryland, and we kept getting Alumni letters. My mom had encouraged me to apply and I did. I began to read about how they played in the DII national championship and were now moving to DI and had just hired a new coach, Dave Cottle.

It was a week before I was due to leave for school and on my birthday, August 15th, I decided I was going to follow in my mother's footsteps and attend Loyola. I called Coach Tierney to explain and apologize. I told him that I wanted to study business and play DI. I repeatedly apologized. I expected him to be upset, but all he said was, "Don't worry about it. I get it. I know EXACTLY what you mean." By the time I arrived in Baltimore a week later, Coach Tierney was already there, coaching a mile down the road at Johns Hopkins University and about to help them to one of the most successful periods in their storied history.

When I arrived at Loyola, Coach Cottle was only 26 years old and his assistants were even younger. The assistants were Dave Huntley, Steve Wey, Bill Sipperly, Henry Cicciarone Jr., and John Tucker would join the staff in my junior and senior seasons. We had 16 or 17 guys that played regularly my freshman year, 10 were freshman and three were transfers from the University of Baltimore, which had just dropped their program. I FOGOed (faced off and got off) my freshman year and ran 1st or 2nd midfield after that, as well as handled face offs. I don't know if Coach had been drinking, but he named me one of our captains for my senior year; I was extremely honored.

This group of young coaches was very demanding and hard charging. We learned to really work, especially on the end line. We did not have depth so we were going to have to be in shape. We ran an indescribable amount. To our detriment Coach read *A Season on the Brink with Bobby Knight* by John Feinstein. However, it did immediately pay off because in our 2nd game that freshman year we had a 4th quarter lead on Syracuse who had just won their first championship the prior year and were ranked #1. This was pretty amazing for such a young staff and so many new players from a team that had been 5-9 a year earlier and lost to teams that many of you probably didn't know played lacrosse. Coach had us immediately competitive with top teams. He did this with next to nothing in facilities and an extremely small budget. We thought the coaches were nuts, but they got us ready and I undoubtedly remember many great times, especially on bus rides back to campus after a big win. I made life long friends, the kind you instantly give a chest bump or a hug to without even thinking about it, even if you haven't seen them for 15 or 20 years. These guys will always be special to me: JC, Woodeye, Cheeker, Toast, Louie, Dicky, Vinnie and John Pfeifer, Tommy McClelland, Jethro, Dahlin, Pat Lamon, Gumbo, Wayno, Kase, Pat Tierney, Steiner, Nages, Rules, Reds, Holt, Gunk, Kronie and Charlie Toomey (currently Head Coach at Loyola). I was recently talked into playing for the Loyolda Grayhounds in Lake Placid. It was great hanging out with some of my teammates and meeting their children. The downside to that is it's been two months since the tournament and I am still hobbling and will be getting scoped soon.

Upon graduating from college, I moved home to Long Island, began working in the city and playing lacrosse for the Long Island Lacrosse Club coached by Tom Postell and John Phillips. We played in numerous Club National Championships and won several. It was fun to take road trips with the guys and play against friends from college, but the best part was always the after party as we would introduce our college mates to our club mates and they would do the same. Practice was the best with the Long Island Lacrosse Club, as the Team would have up to 10 Team USA guys and well over 30 All Americans on it. The best competition that we had all year in some years was in these practices. I was pretty out of shape and over the hill when I played my last 2 years for NYAC, but I was glad to have played for Brian Conroy and Howiie Borkin, and to have made a whole new set of friends, some of whom I will bump into when I get up to the AC for a workout. I've also had great times playing with the Mount Washington Tavern in the Vail, Hawaii and Mardi Gras tournaments.

This brings me to my favorite part of lacrosse: coaching my son Regan, my twin girls Kara and Caitlyn, and their friends. As I mentioned, we live in Huntington, NY on Long Island and my kids play and I coach for the Huntington Village P.A.L. The kids started playing in the clinics before kindergarten. I loved coaching the boys with Fran and Mickey, and with Berta, Christine and John on the girls side. It's also been great coaching against my brother-in-law Chris Scaring, as well as Mike Hannon and Kevin Cook from Manhasset, Jon Reese and Jim Bovich from West Islip, Spives and Vinny Connors from Cold Spring, and Lou Buffalino from Long Beach. The kids have made it all worthwhile. Kevin K., Johnny Shea, JT, TJ, Jeremy, Joe

D., Billy Martin, Ryan Cates and Ryan Casale, Charlie Deegan, Thomas, Aidan, Tim B., Will, Daniel and Regan. On the girls side: Allison, Julia V., Sara, Caroline, Julia M., Sabrina, Caitlyn Concannon, Elizabeth Shea, Eileen K., Megan Quinn, Katie Sappe, Amanda, and my Kara and Caitlyn. Kids, the pleasure is entirely mine. A major benefit to coaching in Huntington was the inspiration provide by the Huntington High School state championship teams and the thrill of following the team's 67 game winning streak. The High School coaches and players also provided instruction and encouragement. My wife and I are especially thankful to Zach Howell, who has mentored my son, Regan for several years. He has inspired my son to strive to reach high academic goals, to behave in a respectful manor in addition to striving for athletic excellence.

My wife and kids love to go to youth tournaments and to Final Fours, but they cannot stand trying to get anywhere because every 10 steps or so we run into someone that I know and share a lacrosse bond with. It takes forever to get anywhere. I tell them that these are not the type of relationships where you can simply pass by without talking to the person; you don't pretend not to see them. This game has given me so much, most importantly being friends, relationships and memories that will last my entire life. I hope that my children and their friends keep playing and coaching because if they do, someday they will then know just how lucky I am.

CHAPTER I:
DRILLIN AND CHILLIN

Johnny wakes up at 9:30AM on a drizzly Saturday morning and hops downstairs to find his parents sitting at their kitchen counter sipping coffee. Johnny's dad is tall at 6'3" and is still in decent shape. He weighs 230lbs., but would like to be 215. Carl Price captained his High School football and lacrosse teams as a senior before going on attend Franklin and Marshall where he faced off as a lacrosse player and co-captained the team his senior year with Eric Schlanger. Janet, Johnny's mother, is still a stunner and a runner as Carl likes to say. Johnny's mom ran sprints out to 400 meters, which was her best event. She captained the Providence College Women's track team and was once named 1st team all Big East. Carl and Julie have been married for 18 years and have three kids. Kim, their eldest, is a 16-year-old drama queen and girly girl who is constantly bothered by any and all in the family. Then there is Johnny, their 13-year-old, and Kate, an 11-year-old. Johnny and Kate are both hardcore laxaholics.

The entire family is eating breakfast except for Kim who is still in bed and will be until at least noon. Johnny has seconds on the scrambled eggs and bacon. His parents sit sipping coffee. Johnny puts the dishes in the sink and says that Kenny is coming by in a little bit and they are going shooting. While he is waiting in the den he pounds out 50 pushups and 50 quick clamps on an imaginary face off opponent. Kenny texts, "b there in 5."

Johnny throws on his North Face, a shell and a blue Under Armour ski hat. He runs upstairs to grab his stick and gloves. He is bounding down the stairs when he realizes he forgot his iPod. As he heads downstairs for the second time, he hears Kenny accepting his mother's invitation for bacon and eggs.

Johnny rolls his eyes at Kenny as he walks into the kitchen. Kenny says, "You don't expect me to let this perfectly good food go to waste. It would be a sin, wouldn't it Mrs. P?" Janet agrees, "Johnny, he is so right on this one, he'll just be a minute."

Kenny finally finishes up and the boys head out for some shooting. They jog down to the high school and find a cage against a baseball back stop. As he points at the backstop Kenny says, "At least this thing is good for something." They both laugh and Kenny goes behind and drives to one side and rolls back at x behind the goal. Johnny times cuts to Kenny's drive.

Kenny can feed him. Johnny's working on catching and shooting on the run and is looking to shoot to the opposite pipe. The two boys are going hard and breathing heavy. They feel the cold air on their lungs.

They switch it up and Johnny takes the balls up top to do some split dodges and feeds. Kenny works on a few stick fakes. It is evident that the kid can finish. After this they work on time and room shooting. Kenny fires rockets with either hand while Johnny has a pretty decent right but the left, not so much.

The boys finish up and decide to hit DiRaimo's for a few slices. They head to town. Heading through the town they pass Dairy Barn and Ryan Kennedy sticks his head out and yells, "Good to see the sticks out! I'll be up there after I get off work around 2:30. You want to meet me?"

Johnny yells, "Yeah man!" and Kenny screams, "Sure!"

They head into DiRaimo's and order two slices each and split a chicken roll. The food doesn't stand a chance and they slurp their sodas until they are gone. Kenny lets out a tremendous burp that causes all the people in line to turn around and laugh.

Kenny says, "Excuuuuuse me!" and the two bone-headed friends howl with laughter. They head back to Johnny's house to chill for a little bit before they meet up with Ryan.

They walk in the door and Kim growls, "If it isn't the two biggest losers in town."

Kenny comes back with, "Kim, why so sweet today? You're usually much nastier."

They head down to the basement and turn on some college hoops. It's Nova-Pitt, they chill a little bit and watch as they two Big East teams battle it out to a 2 point Pitt lead at the half. They talk about how cool it is that the Big East has a lacrosse conference and how they can't wait until mid February when the college games will be on TV. They run up to the kitchen and get some goldfish and gather their stuff again to go meet with Ryan. They shoot up to the school for the 2nd time to find Ryan firing some heat on the goal. It is very impressive. They guess that he is shooting bb's at least in the upper 90's with both hands. The shots seem to blur as they rocket to the corners.

Ryan gives the two boys knuckle bumps and explains that he has the balls spread around and is about 10 to 12 yards in front of the goal. He says that they will flip balls to each other and as the shooter catches it, he will get a command from the flipper of 1(upper) 2(middle) or 3(lower) to the opposite pipe.

First, Ryan goes through the rotation left-handed around the horn shooting high to low and low to high. After completing this lefty, he rotates back around right handed. The boys are completely wowed.

Johnny is up next, he is rotating around left handed. His shots are awkward. He pushes more with his upper body and does not get a good step into it. He only gets off about 3 good lefty shots out of 12. They are all overhand. He does much better coming around righty, putting 10 on cage and 8 on the target that Kenny calls out. Ryan says, "Good job with the right hand, but you have some serious work to do on the left. You can be shooting as well with the left as you do with your right and maybe better by the time you are on varsity. It doesn't happen automatically. You have to do the work."

Kenny is up next and he fires lasers. He is nailing corners with the left, 11 of 12 on target, overhand, side arm, and underhand. He is even better righty. Ryan yells, "Wow!" Somebody has already done a ton of work, MY MAN!"

Next they work on split dodges up top and shooting on the run down the alleys. Ryan says to focus on running at the goal and not fading away, taking away the shooting angle. The boys do well, but Johnny put several wide with both his left and right hands; however, he does get good velocity because he has practiced, uses this momentum, and steps off of the correct foot when he shoots. Ryan points out that he likes to shoot four or five inches inside the pipe to give him room for error and to get more shots on the cage.

It's about 45 degrees, but the three boys have a pretty good sweat going. When Ryan asks, "Johnny, do you want to get some face off work?" Johnny says, "Sure. Kenny you place the ball and say, Down, Set, Go!" Johnny gets set, Kenny brings the ball to Ryan, and places it saying, "Down, Set and Go." Johnny's clamp is like lightning and he cleanly pulls it out behind him and easily scoops it. Ryan is dumbfounded and wants another crack at it right away. It is the same result on the next 3. Finally on the fifth one, Ryan chops over the ball and pushes Johnny's stick off of it and is able to pull the ball behind him to win one. On the next face off, Johnny notices Ryan leaning in and correctly anticipates another chop. Johnny drops his stick backwards and pushes it forward under Ryan's stick. The ball pops forward and he sprints after it. He would've had an easy fast break if it were a game. Johnny takes the next eight in a row and they wrap it up, as it is pretty clear that Johnny is winning them all.

Ryan asks in bewilderment, "How do you do that?"

Johnny replies, "I work on face offs all the time."

Ryan replies, "AHH that work thing. AHHA!"

Johnny says, " I work on it every day, year round."

The boys walk home and as they get to Ryan's house, he says, "We'll do that again, especially those face offs, Johnny. I have some work to do there and before the season."

Johnny and Kenny walk about 30 yards up the hill towards Johnny's house, when Kenny finally looks over his shoulder and says, "BROTHA you CRUSHED him. Can't wait to tell everyone!"

Johnny replies, "No Way! Nobody hears about this, NOBODY!" It's hard for him not to smile.

CHAPTER 2:
INDOOR WINTER BALL

1/13, indoor lacrosse: 7:30AM on a Sunday, all the way out in Farmingville, just to play a team from 2 miles down the road in 7 on 7 non contact lacrosse. The team is a little light on players so they bring Shane McInnis the youngest of three brothers. He is only in 5th grade, but he is really talented and a freak of an athlete. They decide to play him since it is non contact. The non contact part is laughable because the boys are playing The Crush and they will be hitting from the opening whistle and they'll be getting it right back. There are no penalties, but the team with the penalty will have to give up a fast break, which usually winds up in a 1 on 1 with the goalie. Due to the poor lightning, it usually winds up being a tough day on the net minders, the referees start out calling the penalties whenever there is contact, but they will give-up on calling the penalties and they will eventually just let the kids play.

The coaches (Carl, Frank, and Kieran for indoor off season workouts) gather the boys in a huddle and begin giving instructions. Carl (Johnny's dad) says, "Guys, we are playing Bayville and they bring it. It's non contact so no hitting, but be ready to scrap for every groundball. These guys play in Suffolk and I think that they were undefeated last year. So let's get after it from the first whistle. We have a 2-3-2 format and no man down. If there is a penalty, there will be a fast break awarded. Jack and Kenny start on attack. JP you take the face with Ryan and Charlie on the wings. Thomas and Cade you've got the D, and Ronan you're goalie in the first half; Joe you've got the second half. I want to hear a lot of talk out there. Remember, no face offs after goals. So if they score, pick it up and push it. It's a short field so you might be able to hit an attack man on a breakout. If we score, there is no celebrating. We have to get right back on D because the goalie can pick it up right away. Second middies: Bates, RJ, and Eamon you have to be ready to go. We are going to switch on the fly and quickly. Bring it in! Everyone, hands in!" Everyone shouts, "1-2-3 HUSTLE!"

On the opening whistle Johnny quick clamps, pushes the ball forward, and scoops in stride. He has a break. The pole drifts a few steps towards him and leans to him for a split second. Johnny releases a pass to the point attack man, the d-man breaks back and picks off the pass. The pole baited him with a fake slide. His father yells, "Come on Johnny, you've got to draw the man. Make sure he comes to play you or you take it to the HOLE! You know that, c'mon!"

The d-man breaks downfield and is cut off by Charlie Winter. He pushes the pole down the side and lifts the pole's bottom hand as the Bayville defender takes an awkward off balance shot. No problem for Ronan, who catches it and fires a breakout pass to a streaking Ryan McDermot; Ryan catches the pass in stride. At the midfield line he face dodges a defender as he crosses midfield and now has a 3 on 1. Ryan charges into about 8 yards from the goal, draws the man, and hits Kenny Smith about 2 yards left of the crease. Kenny pumps hard opposite pipe and gets the goalie moving across crease, he fires a bouncer near left lower corner. The goalie never had a chance.

All three coaches are screaming, "Get back in the hole!"

The Bayville coach is short and round; Shane quickly nicknames him "Butterball," which has the entire team cracking up. The coaches try not to laugh and even reprimand Shane, but it is pretty funny because he has been screaming and yelling since he hit the parking lot and the man is very round. Butterball screams, "Time out!" The ref tells him that he can have the time out but the clock will keep running, except for the last two minutes of the half or game. Butterball shouts, "I don't care. I want a timeout."

As both teams huddle up, the boys hear Butterball screaming, "You guys better wake up! These guys are kicking your butts all over the field!"

Johnny's dad and Big Kieran are telling the middies and attack to keep going to the goal, draw the slide, and move the ball. Hustle back on D and the attack man should ride like crazy. Keep the pressure up. Frank finishes up with the defense and everyone puts their hand in on top of the coaches hollering, "1-2-3 HUSTLE!"

The ball starts with the Bayville goalie in the crease; he flips the ball to his middies behind the goal and the middie starts up field. Kenny slides off his man to double the ball and the middie drops an easy pass to his defenseman on the wing, then he bursts up field completing the give and go. #42 is heading down the right alley, full steam ahead. Aidan has to slide towards the ball and #42 hit his attack man on the crease, who has all day to stick fake on Ronan and he puts it in, 3-2. Ronan immediately picks it up and fires a breakout pass to RJ who is clearing up the right sideline and gets checked up into the boards. The ref blows the whistle and yells, "This is non contact guys. Fast break: Blue." Butterball screams, "This is lacrosse not badminton!"

RJ gets up a little woozy but shakes it off. He grabs the ball and as the ref blows the whistle he sprints downfield. The point D man slides up to stop the ball, leaving one defender to cover Kenny and John. RJ switches from right to left-hand and as #46 slides to put pressure on him, #34 drifts to his right to cover Kenny, the near attack man. RJ takes a quick step farther left, to create some space, and delivers a pretty pass to John Johnson (JJ), who quick sticks it lower left as the goalie slides across cage, 4-2.

Bayville tries to push the ball up the field and fires a shot on goal with 2 seconds left. Ronan snuffs the shot and the half ends, 4-2 with shouts of, "Rodawg! Way to be! You the man!"

Coach Frank calls out, "Guys everyone get some water or Gatorade. The second half starts in 5 minutes. JoJo put on your chest protector and get warmed up. Toss the ball around and stay loose."

The boys throw it around; JJ catches with Johnny and Kenny. The ref informs the coaches that the second half will start in 2 minutes.

Coach Kieran, Thomas' dad and a monster of a man, yells with a booming voice, "Bring it in boys! Great job getting back in the hole and hustling on groundballs. That is why we are winning, KEEP IT UP. These guys are getting a little chippy out there. Watch it around the boards."

The second half starts with Johnny pulling the face off out to Charlie, who scoops it cleanly and moves the ball to Shane. Shane dodges from the lefty attack slot and beats his man, he looks across crease and raises his stick to pass, which freezes the slide for a second. That is all the time Shane needs, as he turns and fires on goal from 8 yards; upper right corner! Goal!

Butterball shouts, "Darren you cannot hesitate to slide. Slide with the body!" He then proceeds to really humiliate the defenseman. "Are you STUPID or just SCARED!?" When the boy tries to say it's non-contact, he just gets waved off by Butterball who says, "Yea, yea,

yea whatever. Get outta my face. Get to the end of the bench."

The Bayville goalie scoops the ball and hits a middie in the middle of their defensive end. #28 is a big middie and he runs hard over the midfield line where he is jumped by a middie who has just come out of the box on the fly. #28 goes over his head and switches back to his right and is down the alley in a flash. He lets a high bouncer go that beats Joe. Joe was barely warmed up and the ball really bounces off the hard floor. The teams exchange goals and the "good guys" put one more away. Coach Kieran is working the scoreboard and has us ahead 8-4 when Butterball says, "I don't care about the score, but we have one more." Coach responds, "I think that's right, but I don't care…8-4,8-5, 8-8 whatever." Coach was implying that our squad is just trying to get some quality work in before the real season and we don't care about the score. Butterball for some reason takes major offense to this and says, "Don't talk to me like I'm a jackass!" Coach K looks at Carl like, "Is this guy kidding?" It's hysterical, Butterball is 5'7" and a very round 210 lbs. and he is getting in Coach's face. Butterball is screaming, "Are you trying to intimidate me?!" Kieran, trying not to laugh, says, "No, not yet!" Butterball is cursing and yelling about the score and screaming how it is all about the kids and that it's B.S. that our team keeps the score. Carl gets in between Kieran and Butterball because he knows that Kieran can, and just might, drop this guy at any second. As Carl steps up, Butterball's assistant comes strutting over with his shoulders back like Tarzan. The ref, a 17-year-old kid, starts yelling that if anyone says another word than the game is over in 2 seconds. He is visibly shaking in his Nikes. Johnny's dad says, "We are not saying another word to them. We are here to play lacrosse. Are you (Butterball) here to play lacrosse?" He responds, "Yes, we are here to play lacrosse." And that was that. Two more goals by the good guys, one behind the back by Kenny to complete the hat trick making the final score 10-5, counting the goal that we gave them.

On the drive home Carl and Frank are talking about how winter ball is all about tuning up for the season and getting the rust off the kids sticks, but they admit that it felt pretty good beating Butterball and how losing to him would have been a disaster, even though they are a very good team. Carl says, "We jumped all over them and never let them back into it." Then he jokes, "Kenny how many did you have today, 8 (goals) and 5 (assists)? "

Shane chimes in , " Hey guys, Kenny's 'Broch Cinco" and the car erupts in laughter.

Frank adds, "The key to that indoor game is hustling back on D and riding. You get the ball back and you are almost instantly on top of their goal."

The group heads into the diner for a little victory breakfast. At one table, the kids are all imitating Kenny's victory dance after the goal. The fathers shake their heads at the knuckleheads, barking at the boys, "Stay in line" and "Knockoff the horsing around."

The waitress is about 19 years old and very good-looking blonde, long legs and a stunning face. The boys notice and so do their fathers. The men watch the boys as they check her out, waiting for the first inevitable bone headed move by the boys.

She doesn't get halfway through taking the orders when Shane asks if she wants to have coffee when her shift ends. She blushes because she is caught a little off guard by the half sized Romeo and because all the other guys are cracking up. She looks over to the fathers' table for help and they are all laughing as well. Shane's dad apologizes through his own laughter. She turns to Shane and says she would love some coffee but she is working a double and her 6'4" boyfriend is picking her up after work.

Shane replies, "That's cool, we could get to know each other on your coffee break."

The waitress shakes her head and says, "I don't think so, while rolling her eyes, but she is smiling and cracking up a little."

Everyone chows down and shockingly there isn't a food fight. The bill gets paid.

Shane finds the waitress and says, "You forgot to leave your number on the bill." The waitress holds her face in her hand and laughs, "Not this time lover boy."

CHAPTER 3:
MORNING WORKOUTS

At 5:00AM the buzzer sounded and woke John from a deep sleep. It was dark, cold, and the first day of winter break, but he couldn't wait to get going. John would be working-out with Ryan, who lives four doors down from him and is the senior captain and an All American middie for the high school. Ryan is headed to UVA in the fall on a full tuition scholarship and this spring he gets one more chance to lead his varsity team to the NY state championship. It would be Harborview High's first state championship in 12 years.

Johnny jumps into lax shorts, socks, and sneakers. He throws on his "Practice like a champ" tee-shirt and his Under Armour hoodie. John proceeds to brush his teeth, gulp some OJ, and inhale a bagel. He grabs his stick and is out the door and jogging to Ryan's before 6AM.

There is a hop in John's step because he is pumped that Ryan has taken him under his wing. After all, he is only in 8th grade and while he is one of the better kids on his team, Thomas Quinn and Jeremy are the "glory boys" that score most of the goals. Johnny thinks to himself that Thomas and Jeremy would probably give up guitar hero for a year if they could get the chance to practice with Ryan, the best player from around here in at least 15 years.

Ryan sees Johnny bounding down the street and with a wave he signals that he will be right out. He grabs his stick and iPod and pops out of the front door and down the steps. They both break into an easy jog and head towards the high school track. John was so excited that he forgot his mini iPod. He can't believe it! They quickly cover the six blocks to the high school and drop their sticks on the school's news field turf. Ryan tells Johnny that he is lucky because he will get to play on the new turf for the next several years while he only gets one chance. John replies, "I have to wait a year because the Jr. High won't get to play on the turf." Ryan says, "If you keep up the work on the face offs then I think that you'll wind up on JV because coach says that he is moving Kyle Crawford, a tenth grader, up to varsity to run second midfield and handle some work on the face offs." John has a burst of adrenaline as he blurts out, "Do you really think I have a shot?!" Ryan says, "You do if you keep working. Try outs start March 1st."

The boys finish their two mile run and head to the top of the restraining box to work on dodging and shooting on the run. Ryan scoops a ball, jogs about four steps takes a quick little step left, a big step right, and a lightning quick change of direction step to the left, as he switches the stick from his right hand to his left. From this point, Ryan bears down on the goal and fires an overhand lefty rocket that caroms off of the opposite pipe about six inches below the cross bar and into the goal. Johnny yells, "There isn't a goalie in the state that stands a shot of saving that!" Johnny scoops a ball; he wants to impress Ryan. He starts with the ball to his left, puts on a nifty "shake and bake," cuts towards the goal at a 45 degree angle and fires side arm at the opposite corner. The ball whizzes just over the goal. Ryan laughs, "That's cool if you want to look pretty out there, but if you want to be a scorer you have to charge at the goal, not fade away from it. You take away your angle by shooting side arm and fanning out from the goal while on the run. On that, you want to shoot overhand." He added, "Also scorers leave room for error. I shoot for six inches below the crossbar and two or three inches off the pipe. My shot was a little off and I still gave myself a good chance of scoring while you are hoping that the attackman beats the goalie and the D man to the end line." The two take 50 shots with each hand. Johnny hits most of his right handed shots, but the left handers are way too inconsistent. Ryan tells Johnny that if he wants to play DI then he is going to have to work his tail off on that left hand. He tells Johnny that he played three years of summer league using only his left to get it up to speed. Ryan then says, "I have to get to work at Dairy Barn by 8AM, so let's do some face offs and get out of here."

They each get in their stance and work on their moves individually. Both boys use the handle bar style that everyone is using these days and each practices a few different moves, but John's primary move is a quick clamp. The move that he uses 98% of the time with the only difference being whether he pushes the ball forward or pulls it back behind him. Next they line up for a face off against each other. Ryan laughs and says, "I'll say go." Johnny has his weight centered on his feet and off of his hands. He is focusing on the first sound from Ryan. "GO!" Johnny is like lightning with his clamp and quickly has the ball 80% clamped. Now Ryan's strength comes into play and he is too strong for Johnny to fully clamp it, but he has enough of an advantage to put it where he wants and he easily pulls the ball behind him. Ryan can't believe it and shouts, "Do that again!" They line up. Johnny sees Ryan leaning forward weight on his hands. "GO!" Ryan lunges with a fury, but the result is the same. Johnny is too quick and his technique is perfect. Ryan can't believe it. Last year on the varsity he won over 60% of his face offs and this twerp of an 8th grader just smoked him. It wasn't even close.

Ryan says, "I want to know how you do that." John replies, "I work on it all the time with my dad. He faced off in college before they used the motorcycle handlebar grip. My dad says that facing off is 80% quickness; the rest is strength and technique. The quickness gets your stick a little under your opponents and once you have that, you have leverage and leverage is hard to beat. I noticed that you were leaning with your weight on your hands. Keep your weight on your feet with your hands loose so they will be quicker. This will help your move." Ryan says, "WOW! We each learned something today. Same time tomorrow?" John smiles and says, "See you then."

Johnny bursts through the door. His mom is making eggs and his dad is sipping coffee while reading the paper. Johnny is bouncing off the walls as he tells his parents about the shooting drills and the face off; he can barely contain his excitement as he tells them that Ryan thinks that, "He has a good shot of playing on the Junior Varsity!" Johnny locks eyes with his dad who gives him a huge smile and a slow assuring nod. His mom turns around with a big frown on her face and proclaims, "I don't know. Johnny, you only weigh 110 lbs. and that is too thin to go up against some of those monsters!" She looks to her husband for help and says, "I really don't like this." Carl just smiles (he knows that their hard work is paying off and he knows how excited his Johnny is.) Mom snickers, "You're both sick!" and storms off. Carl and Johnny look at each other and laugh, but not too loudly because they can tell that she is smoking mad about this on one.

CHAPTER 4:
HANGIN WITH THE BRO'S

John's phone rings blasting his favorite tune. He sees that it is Kenny calling in and he picks up, "Hey Kenny, what up kid?"

Kenny, "You wanna shoot with JP and I, then catch the movie at 2:15?"

John says "Cool! I'll see you at the high school."

Kenny, "We'll be there around noon."

John, "I'll see ya guys then."

Up at the school, the sun is actually peeking through the clouds and it's looking like a pretty good day. There are 25 or 30 kids up there firing shots on one end of the field. Tunes are cranking and people are getting fired up for the season, which will start in two weeks.

Johnny arrives and Kenny and PJ are already down at the far end of the field, dragging a goal to a spot in front of the backdrop net. The guys all low five, chest bump, and knuckle up. Kenny says, "Charlie, Ryan, Ronan and a few other guys might show in a few." RJ shows up with Charlie

Kenny: Cool you brought some tunes, get them blasting."

The five teammates and best buds since kindergarten are fired up for the upcoming season. RJ goes behind the net and is feeding cutters to both sides. They both alternate their cuts between left and right. Johnny focuses on aiming three inches inside the opposite pipe. He doesn't get as many corners as the others, but he is satisfied that this will help him score more goals.

Next the boys work on side arm cranks from the wing and up top. Johnny can do this pretty well, but like most of the others he doesn't have a crank with the left. Only Kenny can gun it with a set side arm shot with either hand. RJ can crank with his left but he's a lefty. Johnny and the other middies work on a move from up top where they step in as if they are going to let one fly side arm righty, but at the last second they pull a face dodge, quickly switch to the left sprint down the pipe and shoot from 8 or 9 on the run to the opposite pipe.

After almost 2 hours the boys head to Johnny's to drop off their sticks before they leave for the movies. The boys bounce up Johnny's steps, leave their sticks on the porch, and through the door. "Hey Mrs. Price" "Hello boys. How are we doing today? Can we get you guys some lunch?"

"No mom. We are grabbing slices and heading to the movies." Johnny said.

Janet asks," What are you seeing boys?"

Kenny says, "We are going to see the new horror movie. It's suppose to be really gruesome."

Janet just rolls her eyes as the boys head out the door.

The boys hop into DiRaimo's Pizzeria, the only pizza place in town that's still called a pizzeria. They pound two or three slices each with iced teas and head down the block to the movies. They get tickets, popcorn, Skittles and Sour Patch Kids. All set. They are lucky enough to find a group of seats together.

After the movie, they head out of the theater and cross the street to go home. Ryan sees the boys crossing and steps out of Dairy Barn and yells to Johnny "Same time tomorrow, Johnny?"

Johnny says, "You got it Ry. See you at 6."

The guys want to know what's up, so Johnny tells them and they all want to know if they can come. Johnny says that he will text Ryan and ask him. He does and Ryan responds that if they can get up and keep up, it's fine with him.

The guys are all pumped. They walk home to Johnny's and tell his mom that they are going to be working out with Ryan the next morning. She mocks "OMG" with a squeal, "Not THE Ryan Kennedy, idol and envy of every boy in town and heartthrob of all the girls, All American middie and straight A student!" She laughs and shakes her head. Janet then says, "That is pretty nice of him to work with you boys."

Johnny eats dinner with his parents, Kim, and Caity. Kim breaks his chops every chance she gets and she is definitely good. He enters into his log: 200 pushups,

2 mile run, 4 x 100 yard sprints, 8-40s and 10-10s, 2 sets of 100 lefty and 100 right-handed shots, 100 clamps and 20 live face-offs. He needs more live face offs. If Ryan has to leave for work again, he will have to find somebody to give him a few more reps.

Day 2: The Boys meet on Johnny's porch at 5:55AM. Everyone has their stick and iPod. They bounce down to Ryan's house. He is waiting for them and they are off to the High School, 2 miles on the track. Johnny and Ryan lead the way. Charlie and RJ are the first to fall behind, then JP and Kenny fall back after about three laps.

Everyone finally gets done and Ryan says, "On the end line." This is met with a loud chorus of groans. Ryan continues, "I drove down Northern Boulevard the other day and there had to be 150 kids practicing in Manhasset. I saw Huntington out there yesterday and you know West Islip, Garden City, and Northport have been going hard all winter. God only knows what they are doing out in Shoreham. YOU HAVE GOT TO WANT IT! ON THE END LINE!" The boys suck it up. The100s almost kill Charlie but he gets through them. He bails midway through the 40s, as does RJ. The rest of the guys make it through and Charlie and RJ make it back for the 10 yarders.

Shooting drills: Balls are flying everywhere but in the goal. Besides Ryan, Kenny is the only one finding the net consistently. Johnny scores on about half of his shots; his left is improving. The guys are getting their second wind and the tunes are giving them a little extra energy. Everyone seems to step up their shooting. Ryan and Johnny pair off for face offs. 50 clamps each simultaneously. Johnny says, "Remember your weight on your feet not on your hands." They get in about 35 live face offs. Johnny wins 26. They all leave the field exhausted but excited to be back the next day.

5:45AM the next morning Johnny wakes and gulps down some OJ between bites of a buttered cinnamon raisin bagel. He looks outside; it is wet, windy, and cold. He wonders how many of the guys will show. 5:55AM and no one has arrived. He grabs his stick and heads out the door, tunes pumping, and hoodie on. He gallops down the block to Ryan's house. Ryan is ready. They start to head out but as Ryan joins Johnny he points down the block with a lacrosse stick. They wait a minute. It's Kenny. Kenny says, "Ya didn't think I was coming, did ya?"

Johnny replies, "I thought you rolled over with the blankets up to your chin like the rest of the clowns."

The three brave the cold and bang out their two mile run and sprints. They work on skipping their shots off the wet turf. The rain is turning to sleet as Ryan and Johnny start their face offs. Kenny helps by setting the ball and yelling, "Go." Ryan is improving and finding a way to counter Johnny's initial move and use his size and strength to his advantage, but Johnny still wins 22 of 35. They call it a day.

The boys jog home with Ryan breaking off at his house and Kenny and Johnny continuing to his own.

Kenny says, "Man, nice job on those face offs! I know that you're good, but I didn't think that you could beat Ryan, day after day. That's awesome!" Johnny says, "Yeah, I've been working on it a lot with my dad. I won 26 yesterday, Ryan is getting better. He'll catch and pass me soon."

For Kenny, Ryan and Johnny, the routine continues for the rest of the winter vacation. The rest of the guys join them on Thursdays and Fridays, but stay up too late Friday night while sleeping over Charlie's to get out of bed for the workouts.

CHAPTER 5: CAPTAINS PRACTICE

It's the last week in February and everyone is back to school. There is a lot of chatter about lacrosse tryouts coming up in a week. Johnny gets a text from Ryan: YO GUY, WHATTUP? WE ARE HAVING CAPTAINS PRACTICE AFTER SCHOOL. TELL KENNY AND THE BOYS TO GET UP THERE…NO EXCUSES!

Johnny tells the guys and they are all fired up to be working with the varsity. Johnny is itching to get to practice, he can't wait. At lunch JP, Kenny, Ryan, Charlie, and Ronan sit together. They are pumped, but a little worried about going up against defensemen like Mike Ferrarra (6'4", 230lbs), Wally Jantzen (6' 215lbs) and Teddy Smith (6'2", 210lbs.)

Ronan isn't worried and says, "That's nothing, I'm going to have Ryan firing on me at 100 mph, with either hand. However, I will deal with that pain, if it gets me pointers from Danny C." Danny C is the highest recruited goalie in the country who has just decided to take a ride to Notre Dame.

Classes finally end and the guys quickly gear up and head to the turf. The junior high school is on the same property as the high school, so everyone gets to the turf in a hurry. Guys are loosening up and playing catch while the goalies are getting warmed up. After about 10 minutes of this, Ryan calls everyone to the middle of the field:

> Guys, this is the last go 'round for myself and the other seniors and we'd like to get the chance to go out on top. In order to do that we need everyone here pulling in the same direction. We need everyone focused on the team goal, not individual goals. We may have to overcome obstacles and we will, but we do not want to create obstacles. By this I mean getting in trouble off the field, in school, or in town. No fights. No off-field injuries. Nobody drinking or doing drugs. We've been working with weights, running, and shooting on our own. It starts as a team right here, right now. I am committing to leaving it all on the field every practice and every game. If we all do that we have a very good chance of doing some big things. I AM TALKING STATE CHAMPS! It's what we dreamed of since P.A.L.! Everybody put your sticks in, 1-2-3 BE THE BEST!

The whole squad takes a universal lap around the outside of the school's property. The lap is about a mile and a half. Then everyone breaks into lines for stretching and calisthenics. Ryan, Danny Corwin, and Teddy Smith are the varsity captains and they lead the group through stretching, sit ups, pushups, and jumping jacks. Then everyone breaks off for line drills. After the line drills the players break down into groups, attack and defense together, and then the middies. There were six goals scattered in different corners of the field. The first drill was 1on 1. Johnny was up against Scott Ehrlich, a sophomore with pretty good speed. Johnny put on his best split dodge right to left, got a step on him, and bore down on the goal. Ehrlich managed to get a slight lift on Johnny's bottom hand just before he let it go. Three inches inside the pipe and below the crossbar, but not enough on it. Easy save for Danny. Johnny trots back to play defense. He breaks down in his defensive stance and prepares to cover Cam, a short, speedy middie with a good stick. Cam jogs up, head fakes, stutter steps left, and comes back right as Johnny starts dropping in and tries to connect with a poke check. He swivels his hips and runs with Cam down the side, keeping his stick in front of him as Cam pulls his stick back to shoot. Johnny leans his body on him and shoves him down the side, taking away his angle and forcing him to take an off balance shot. Dano is all over the shot, catches it, yells "Break," and hits Johnny over the shoulder, heading up towards midfield.

Next up are 2 on 2s. Johnny watches as Kenny and Zach Hutchings team up against two varsity

D men. Zach begins with the ball and heads towards a pick that Kenny is setting at X. They work the pick and roll perfectly. Kenny pivots, catches the pass from Zach, and comes around the cage lefty. He gives a quick fake to the opposite pipe and gets Danny C moving across the cage. Kenny sees the opening and buries the shot in the near upper corner as the team hoots and whistles. Someone yells out, "SHOWTIME." Johnny just shakes his head and laughs.

Practice is over pretty quickly, about an hour and 15 minutes. The guys get on the end line and finish with 10 full field sprints. Most of the guys are dying. Johnny and Kenny are having no problems. They're glad that they have been working out and notice that Ryan is obliterating his group and passing the group in front of him. He is going all out on every one of them. The team runs these captain's practices Monday through Friday for the week before the tryouts start. Ryan has put in a good word to Coach Pomper about several of the 8th graders that he thinks can play Junior Varsity, especially noting Kenny and Johnny. Coach agrees to allow them to tryout and to give them a look.

CHAPTER 6:
TRYOUTS

Johnny, Kenny, and Carl are watching TV when Carl asks, "Are you ready for these tryouts tomorrow?"

Johnny explains to him that he is so nervous about having a bad day and not playing well. Carl tells him that he is going into this with the wrong frame of mind. This is a great opportunity with no downside. If Johnny gets moved down to the middle school team then that is where he is supposed to be and that it doesn't mean that his lacrosse career is over, just that he'll have to wait a little longer to be a star for the Harborview Hawks. On the other hand, if he makes the squad then that it is a huge opportunity that would make any 8th grader proud. His father tells him to play with aggression and determination and to put any mistakes behind him quickly. If he goes hard right away, he will get the jitters out and be fine. He should be confident due to all the preparation he has done.

Coach P walks out onto the track and says, "Gentlemen on my whistle you have a mile. You have 6 minutes to complete it or you will have 3 extra sprints after our normal sprints." He blows the whistle and they are off.

The team runs through line drills: 1 on 1s, 2 on 2s and they get down to scrimmaging, 6 on 6. Johnny is all over the field and pouncing on loose balls as soon as they hit the ground. Whenever he scoops a gb (groundball), he turns away from pressure and moves it to an open man quickly. He also knows every players' dominant hand and tenaciously tries to force his opponent to their weak hand whenever he defends them. After a week of practice, he feels as if he is definitely in the top 6 to 8 middies on the team and feels confident that he can handle the speed and size of the older players. He knows that he is pretty much out hustling everyone on the field.

The team is showering after Friday's practice and the locker room is buzzing as they have a three way scrimmage the next week. Johnny and Kenny are finishing up in the locker room; Kenny has hair slicked back and is impersonating Elvis. He couldn't look more ridiculous.

"Hey Johnny," Coach P calls out. "Can I see you in my office?"

Johnny strolls in nervously. Coach points to the chair and says, "Take a seat." Johnny feels it. He is getting cut. Here comes the ax.

Coach begins, "Look, I have 37 kids on the team and I can only keep 28. You are doing great, but I am probably going to send you down to the JR high team, where you'll get a lot more run and be a star. You are as good as many of the kids on the team, but to keep an

8th grader in a 10th graders spot you have to be better than they are by a lot. You know, be a big impact guy, immediately. Win some games for us. Right now I can make a case for Kenny and you are good enough to be on our team, but" a long hesitation follows. "Look you have worked your tail off! And I know we haven't seen you face off a lot this week. I see how hard you run and work at everything you do." MORE SILENCE... Coach P says, "Look, I'm not trying to put pressure on you, but I want you to know what you are up against. Play your best and we'll see what happens in the scrimmages."

Johnny barely talks at dinner that night. He can't get to sleep. He gets out of bed a few times and pops his clamp move. Kim screams at him, "Knock it OFF! I have to get to sleep."

The next day is a scrimmage against Hills and St. Anthony's, two of the strongest programs on Long Island.

At dinner Johnny was quiet as his dad asked if he was up for the scrimmages and what he knew about Hills and St. A's. He barely grunted out that yeah, he was up for it and "Dunno much about either." He headed up to his room right after dinner but knew that he'd never get to sleep.

CHAPTER 7:
THE SCRIMMAGES

Johnny didn't need the alarm clock to wake him up today.

He pops out of bed and is off to school in a flash. He bangs out 25 clamps and 25 rakes. He then proceeds to shoot 20 on the run righty and lefty. The school day seemed to drag on for eternity. Class finally ends and the guys head to the locker room. Johnny is extremely nervous and this continues on the short bus ride to Half Hollow Hills North. It will be a three way scrimmage with Hills North and St. Anthony's JV squads.

Coach P calls the squad in and says, "Men, we have a half against Hills and then we will have a 10 minute break, turnaround and go at it with St. Anthony's. We want to play hard and play smart! Be smart and AGGRESSIVE! All in 1-2-3." Everyone yells, "BE THE BEST!"

Johnny is completely focused as he gets ready to face off against the Hills middie. He is short and thick, but Johnny is too busy focusing to notice. He tells himself to be light on the hands, concentrate on the first sound, and to explode on the very first sound from the whistle. The ref calls them in and says, "Down, Set" and blows the whistle. Johnny explodes into his clamp and is able to pop it out to the side and get it himself. He pops a pass over the shoulder of the converging long pole coming in from the wing. It is an easy catch for the wide open Zach Hutchins. He settles it into the box as Johnny runs to the box to shouts of, "Nice face, Johnny!" and "Way to go, bro! All day my man, All DAY!"

It doesn't take Kenny long to make an impact as he buries a side arm crank from 12 yards on the right wing. The shot catches the inside of the pipe on the upper right side about 4 inches below the crossbar. 1-0, the good guys. Johnny just shakes his head and smiles, knowing that Kenny likes to score the first one of the game on an outside crank. He has seen this since second grade. He hasn't lost his confidence up on the JV.

Johnny pulls the next face off back between his legs where it is an easy groundball for Billy. The Hawks work the ball around the horn until it gets to Bobby Mills up top. They set an iso (isolation dodge) up top for Bobby. He beats his man and draws the slide. Aidan Quinn sees his defender looking to help on the crease and sneaks around the goal, where he receives a nice feed from Bobby and slips the ball over the goalie's off stick shoulder. 2 nil. Johnny scoops and wins the next face off himself. He runs through a little pressure and gets the ball to Aidan, who has popped out on the left side. Aidan moves the ball to X behind the goal. Kenny receives the pass and drives hard to the opposite side, the right side. He draws a crowd and finds Billy McDermott streaking off of a high pick set by the crease attackman. Billy catches it, cradles once, and fires an on-the-run bouncer off the right pipe. The ball is picked up and cleared by a Hills' long pole. The Hills offense wastes no time. They get the ball to a shifty attackman behind the goal. He drives hard right, comes back left, and beats his man with a finalizer back to his right and wraps a shot around Billy Timlin to make it 2-1. On the ensuing face off Johnny puts a cap on any momentum that Hills has by clamping the ball and pulling it back to Jake, his long pole on the wing. Jake scoops the ball on the dead run. He is challenged by the Hills' middies, but has a full head of steam and flies by them. He has a lane down the right alley and Jake doesn't hesitate. He gets about five steps inside the restraining line and fires a laser that goes over the Hills goalie's left shoulder; 3-1 and the Hawks bench goes berserk.

Johnny clamps the next face and is able to pop it out forward and get it himself. He flies with the ball into the box. The Hills defender starts his slide to Johnny and Johnny moves it to point, but as he does this the defender steps into the lane and knocks the pass down. The defender successfully baited Johnny, but luckily Jake is there to grab the loose ball and bails Johnny out of trouble. Johnny runs to the box to find Coach P waiting for him. He says, "Son, you have to make him COMMIT TO YOU or YOU TAKE IT TO THE GOAL. Do you understand me?" Johnny nods his head.

Coach then tells him that he has done a good job, but they are going to put Bobby MacDonnell in to take a few and that he should be ready to go for Anthony's. The Hills squad gets a few possessions and battles back to make it 4-3, but Nick McInnis catches a feed on a fast break and fakes high and shoots low for a late goal that puts the scrimmage away for the Hawks.

Next up for the Hawks are the St. Anthony's Friars. Johnny will be battling on the faces offs with Jerry Nolan. Jerry is the older brother of Kevin Nolan. Kevin is Johnny's buddy from his Long Island Express summer team. Jerry bumps knuckles with Johnny and greets him, "What's up punk? Are you ready for a whuppin?" Johnny just shakes his head.

The teams are lined up to start. Johnny squares up and the ref says, "Down, Set" and blows the whistle. Johnny clamps and is a little quicker than Jerry, but cannot fully clamp the ball. They battle for a second or two, and since Johnny is slightly more clamped over the ball, he decides to push in with all his might and pull it out. The ball barely trickles out in the direction that he pulls it, but it is just enough for him to get the ball. He runs it into the box and hits Aidan who has used a V cut to get open and get the ball. He runs back to the box knowing that it will be a much tougher battle at the face off X than the scrimmage vs. Hills.

The teams are tied at 2 apiece when Jerry Nolan split dodges right to left and rips a rocket to the upper right corner to make it 3-2. Johnny has won 3 of 4 face offs, but Coach P puts Bobby in for the next face off. Jerry clamps it and pushes the ball forward for a fast break. He hits the point man early and receives a return pass and continues to the goal. He finishes the give and go with a high bouncer that puts St. A's up 4-2.

Coach P walks over to Johnny and shouts, "Son, we NEED the ball! GO GET THE BALL!" Johnny races out to take the face off. He finds a new face off middie waiting. He wins this cleanly and pulls it back to Jake. The Hawks fire several shots that miss the mark, but they back up the cage and retain possession. Aidan Quinn receives the ball on the left wing and his defender comes out to play him. Aidan draws him out further and blows by him just as the D man lunges to check him. Aidan sprints to the goal, fakes a pass to the crease that makes the slide hesitate, and that is all the time and room he needs as he buries a low bouncer off pipe to make it 4-3.

Johnny heads out for the face and is met this time by Jerry. The refs announce that only 40 seconds remain in the scrimmage. The face off men get down on the refs' call. Johnny notices that Jerry's stick doesn't even touch the ground and he anticipates a chop check, where Jerry lifts his stick over the ball and pushes Johnny's stick out of the way. The ref blows the whistle, Johnny drops his stick backwards until it is flat to the ground, and pushes forward and under Jerry's stick. It is the perfect counter move and Johnny is off racing after the ball. He scoops it on the run. He pumps a fake pass to the point and keeps heading to the goal. The slide comes and so does the second slide, so Johnny skips it to Kenny who is arching around the crease. The third slide never gets there and Brocho Cinco buries it lower right before anyone can bat an eye. The scrimmage ended 4-4. Later on, Coach would laugh when one of the parents said, "We won that one 4-4 and it wasn't even too close."

Johnny stared out the window as the bus slowly pulled away. He was oblivious to the laughter and chatter that consumed the bus. He nudged Kenny and asked, "Do you think I made it?"

Kenny said, "My man, you played great! If Brocho is making the decision, you're in."

Johnny replied, "Too bad you're not making the decision. As for you, I would highly doubt that you are on the team when cuts are posted."

Kenny looked at him with a wide-eyed frown, at which time Johnny says, "They probably put you straight up to the varsity to name you captain over Ryan." The two friends crack up.

Tommy Smith, the team wise guy, is hanging over their seat and out the window. He is literally howling at a group of girls waking on Main St. He yells "Yo Momma, you wearing space pants? Cause your AZZZ is outta this world." The bus roars with laughter. The smallest girl there yells, "Smitty, you are a complete LOOOOOSER!"

He turns red and looks at Johnny because he realizes that it's Kim and Caity, Johnny's sisters.

Johnny nods his head and says, "That's right, she's in 5th grade."

The bus explodes in laughter. Coach P shakes his head and yells down the bus, "Smitty will be running on the track long after tonight's dance is over."

The bus pulls into the school parking lot and Coach P says that he will post the final roster on Monday. He also says that drinking at all, even once, is strictly forbidden and that anyone caught drinking will be kicked off the squad.

CHAPTER 8:
MAKING THE SQUAD

There is a lot of horsing around and towel snapping going on in the locker room, but everyone is in a hurry to get out and to the dance.

Kenny and Johnny are the last to leave; Johnny doesn't want to. They both grab their gear and head out. As they pass Coach P's office, he calls to them and waves them in. "Sit down, you guys played great today. Kenny with 10 and 6."

Kenny says, "Coach it was 7 and 3."

Coach P smiles and says, "Is that all, Mr. Brocho Cinco? Maybe you didn't play so well then. Johnny coming into today, I didn't know how I could keep you on the team, but you were key in a close one and gave us key possession in the second one that put us in control. You were 9 for 11 at the X. Without that, we have problems. Boys, welcome to the JV. Be ready to work. You can't tell anyone until I post the squad on Monday. Now get outta here!"

The boys walk the four blocks to Johnny's house. They were exhausted getting off the bus, but now they are exhilarated. Kenny gives Johnny knuckles as Johnny breaks off to his house.

Johnny walks through the door and greeted by his mom, "Great game Johnny!" as she hugs him, Johnny winces.

Mom says, "Are you alright? I knew you shouldn't be playing with those older, bigger kids."

Johnny's dad comes up and puts his hand gently on Johnny's shoulder, "Are you okay?"

Johnny says, "C'mon mom, this ain't ballet. And you're too late anyway cause I'M ON THE TEAM!" No sooner than he says it does he realize that he has a problem with this blabber mouthed sister, who is going to the dance.

Dad shouts "You are the man! That's great!"

His mom looks worried but she gives a kiss as she says, "Congratulations!"

Blabbermouth says, "I'm late, kisses mom and dad," and heads out.

Dad shouts, "11:30, No later!"

"No problem, dad."

Johnny slips out and jogs after her. Kim says, "What do you want, loser?" He says, "Hey, here is an extra $20. Look I need a favor, no one can find out that I'm on the team until it is posted on Monday, NO ONE! And if no one finds out until Monday afternoon then Mom and Dad won't have to know about your cursing out Tommy Smith at the top of your lungs on Main Street today, got it?"

Kim snaps, "Got it loser." As she snags the 20 dollar bill without breaking stride. "Now beat it. It's bad enough that you will be playing with all my friends and I'll probably even have to watch you play." She disappears down the block and Johnny heads home.

Monday rolls around and Johnny is buzzing. He can't wait for school to end and to head over to the locker room. After a day that feels unusually long, Johnny meets Kenny and they head over to the lacrosse locker room at the high school.

Johnny sees a line outside of Coach P's office. Coach is in his office talking to the guys that got cut from the team. Three of them are freshman and will be put back down on the freshman team, two sophomores are cut outright, and there are three injuries. Coach will have to figure out what to do with them down the road when a few of the guys get back from injuries. Johnny and Kenny walk downstairs to the locker room. Everyone is fired up. Ryan K. walks up and good naturedly punches the two 8th graders on the shoulders. "Nice job," he yells. "Now get dressed and get out there to set up the goals!" Everyone cracks up.

The guys all dress. Johnny and Kenny along with a few other guys set up four goals for the JV and Varsity. Everyone lines up on the track. Coach P says, "Men, we have the mile. 6 minutes or we will have extra sprints at the end of practice. Get it done." He blows the whistle and the team takes off. Everyone but Bobby Curry and Chris Samuelson finish in under 6 minutes. Samuelson finishes in 6:08 and Bobby Curry in 6:42. Johnny is happy to have finished in 5:44, but there will be extra sprints because the whole team did not make it.

Coach P calls the squad together. "Gentlemen, in two days we have our first game of the year against Holy Family. They are an up-and-coming program. We need to focus and outwork these guys. On D we need to talk and work as a unit, get all over ground balls, and get it out of our end. On O, we need to take care of the ball, play our game, and finish when we get our opportunities. Let's get into cals."

The team zips through cals and line drills with an obvious buzz. They proceed to go over riding and clearing, man up and man down, multiple substitutions, and a few offensive sets. They finish with a feeding and shooting drill, while the defense works on cross field, passing, and breakouts. Practice is quick and ends around 4:45PM.

Coach P tells Johnny and Bobby Mac to join the varsity guys to work on face offs.

They run over and join Ryan and three other face off guys: Kyle Cook, Steve Timson and Owen Smith.

Coach Sipperly pairs them off and says that two guys will face and the winner stays. The loser gets on the end of the line. The first two to face are Ryan and Kyle. Coach Sipp blows the whistle and Ryan cleanly clamps it, pulls it between his legs and scoops.

Coach Sipp, "Nice Ryan! Kyle, end of the line."

Ryan makes quick work of Steven Owens. It's Johnny's turn. He gets his stance down: handle-bar grip with his right hand at the throat of the stick and the left hand 14 inches down the shaft with his weight on his feet and off his hands. Johnny gets a good jump at the first sound of the whistle. He gets a quick clamp and blasts his shoulder into Ryan. He pulls the ball to the left and pounces on it.

Coach Sipp yells, "Whoa! Way to go there Mr. JV! End of the line Mr. All American." The other kids in line scream and yell, "OOOOH BABY!"

Johnny wins the next four face offs on three clamps and a chop. He gets set for the rematch with Ryan. By this time several more JV and Varsity players have gathered around.

Coach Sipp is laying it on pretty thick, "C'mon Ryan! You are our 'CAPTAIN.' You're not going to let 'Johnny the 8th grader' beat you again, are you?!"

The guys that have stuck around to watch erupt with laughter.

Johnny gets set and glances over at Ryan who is snorting furiously. He anticipates that Ryan is going to chop check and try to out muscle him. The whistle blows. Johnny is right and Ryan chops, but Johnny is quicker. He drops his head backwards to the ground and rakes forward under Ryan's stick, the ball shoots forward as Johnny sprints after it. Ryan's momentum is going forward in the opposite direction of the ball plus he glances off Johnny and is totally off balance.

The crowd roars as Johnny easily scoops the uncontested groundball. Coach Sipp shouts, "I've seen enough! Way to go JV! Varsity carries the goals to the Shed!"

Kenny screams, "That's my boy! We are BOYZZ!"

Kenny and Johnny shower up, and after loitering in the locker room for a while, they are finally ready to go. Ryan is long gone. He's not walking home with them today.

Dinner is on the table. Mrs. Price invited Kenny to stay. Kenny quickly agrees as he spots the chicken parm on the table.

Jen starts boasting that her team beat South Shore 13-8 and all about her hat trick. "Dad tell 'em about my second goal, when I split the two defenders and stuck the corner," she says.

Johnny sarcastically says, "Who do we have here Caity Price or Jen Adams?"

Mr. K shoots Johnny a look and says, "Easy there. How was your practice today?"

Johnny, "OK."

Kenny, "WHAT!? Are you kidding? OK?" He then proceeds to tell every detail of the face off competition including all the heckling and 'oohs' and 'aahs'.

Dad says, "Wow that's exciting!"

Mom says, "Poor Ryan."

Johnny says, "Mom we don't have to feel sorry for Ryan. We are all dreaming of getting to where he is already."

Mom replies, "I know Johnny, but Ryan has always been such a nice guy, especially to you, right?"

Johnny says, "Definitely mom."

CHAPTER 9:
GAME DAY

Johnny's alarm blares at 6:00AM. He doesn't hit snooze today, he bounces out of bed, is in and out of the shower. He throws on his jeans, an Under Armour tee, and a pair of shoes. He bounces down the stairs.

His mom says, "Good morning" and gives him a kiss. His dad looks up from the paper and asks if he is ready for his first game.

He eats a banana and gulps OJ out of the container. His mom smacks him and says, "Knock it off, that's disgusting."

Johnny says, "The container is coming with me mom. Gotta go!"

Mom, "Wait for your English Muffins!"

They pop up, he butters them, and wraps them in a paper towel as he grabs another banana. He throws on his North face, scoops his backpack and stick, and is out the door.

"Good luck!" his parents yell after him.

Johnny is cruising down the street wolfing down the English muffin. His phone buzzes and it's Kenny texting, "Yo where are you!? Get up to the field." Johnny picks up the pace.

Johnny comes around the corner of the school and sees Kenny working a face dodge and shot. He jogs to the corner of the field and drops his backpack. Kenny lobs a pass over the goal to him; Johnny catches it, spinning behind the goal, switching it from left to right on the roll, and snapping a pass to Kenny, who is cutting across the crease. Kenny receives the pass and one times a bouncer off the lower left pipe. He hollers, "All day baby! We better get going, class is about to start."

Classes seemed to take forever and Johnny's thoughts kept drifting to the upcoming game. He was finally in American History, his last class of the day. He slipped into his desk and was greeted by Allie, "Game day, huh? My brother says that is going to be pretty tough. Good luck. Kim, Jen and I are going to the game."

Johnny murmurs, "Thanks."

History drags and drags. Johnny cannot focus. The clock eventually gets to 2:45PM, but seems to be stuck there. The last five minutes of the day seem like five hours. FINALLY the bell rings.

Johnny books it, even though Mr. Campotello is reading out the homework assignment. He is in the locker room within two minutes and gears up. He is first on the field. He goes through 25 clamps and 25 rakes, followed by 15 groundballs. Kenny and RJ pop out of the locker room. They feed each other in a triangle, moving to the ball, roll to the outside, switch hands and move the ball.

Pre-game, Coach P calls everyone in. "Gentlemen, first game, Holy Family Crusaders. Let's get after groundballs all day! WE MOVE THE BALL! When you get an opening, set your feet and let it go EVERY TIME, unless someone has a better shot than you, then you move the ball EVERY TIME!"

Coach P yells, "Captains, line em up for cals!" Everyone lines up, spaces out in 5 lines, 5 deep with Vince and Pete leading the stretches.

They work through line drills with everyone bouncing and chirping. The team is very fired up. Kenny knuckle bumps Johnny and says, "Play hard and with confidence."

Johnny replies, "You got it, brother!"

They are working over the shoulder catches, where they turn and throw it to the far line. On Johnny's turn he breaks out and catches it over his left shoulder. He then fires a lefty pass and it bounces at Vince's feet. He yells, "C'mon Johnny, we have a game today!"

Coach P pulls the team into the huddle and barks, "Gentlemen this is what we have been working and waiting for. Our first opponent: The Holy Family Crusaders. You need to step up, get over any butterflies that you have, and make it happen! Play with your head and play with confidence. I want to see 60 minutes of all out hustle and unselfish play! All hands in…" "1-2-3! BE THE BEST!"

Johnny is going out for the first face off. The teams line up. The ref gives instructions and tells the goalies to cross over and shake hands, and then everyone else crosses over, bangs gloves and says, "Good luck."

Johnny lines up for the face off. Vince and Smitty are on the wings. His opponent from Holy Family is #24; he is about 5'10" and thick.

The ref says, "I am going to place the ball on the ground, you guys will not touch the ball. I'll make sure that the sticks are straight, back up, and blow the whistle."

The guys get down. The ref places the ball and says," Down!" backs away and blows the whistle. Johnny clamps, so does #24, but Johnny is quicker. He cleanly pulls it behind him to Vince who scoops it and jogs the ball into the offensive end. Mission accomplished. Johnny heads off to the substitution box. The team settles the ball and works it once around with the guys breaking in and then out to receive the ball.

The ball rotates from up top to the wing then X behind. Kenny catches it from the wing attackman, switches from left to right while he spins to the outside, and drives hard to GLE (goal line extended.) The slide comes early and hard. Kyle cuts off slide a pick from Vince, he cuts to the opposite pipe. Kenny hits him with a feed, but Kyle has it in the wrong hand. He tries to catch spin and shoot but he is checked. Turnover. Holy Family clears the ball and settles in O. They pop it around once and clear through for a sweep. Their big middie sweeps to his right and lets a rocket fly high to high stick side from about 12 yards. Billy sees that all the way and sucks it up no problem screaming "BREAK!"

RJ was covering the shooter and breaks out immediately. He has 7 or 8 yards on his man. Billy hits him in stride. RJ pushes it for a 4 on 3 break; he hits the point man from there down to Kenny, who fires it over to Joe. Joe fakes high as the goalie slides across the goal and shoots low around the goalie. 1-zip.

Johnny trots out to X. He hears his dad scream, "C'mon Johnny, YOUR BALL!"

Johnny and stubby #34 set down, the ref blows the whistle. Johnny quickly clamps and pulls it to the side. #34 comes from behind and tries to go over his back. He misses and Johnny is off to the races. He tries to get it to point, but too soon the big long pole holds on the point attackman as Johnny is staring at him the whole way and looking to pass. He has to pull it out as the defensive wingman has caught up to him. The break is over. Johnny runs to the box. Coach P grabs him, "You have to make someone play you. Draw the slide. Keep it up at X."

Back on the field, Kyle has the ball up top. He skips the ball to Kenny on the wing when he sees that Kenny's defender has stepped inside a little to help on a slide. Kenny catches and fires high to low off side nicking the pipe, 2-zip.

Quick clamp again, this time Johnny pulls it between his legs and behind him. Tommy is flying in from the wing for the ball with the Crusaders middie right on him. Johnny sticks his shoulder into the middie as Tommy scoops it. The wing middie explodes through Johnny, knocking him down and completely head over heels. It is enough to free Tommy to get the ball. The bench roars as Johnny runs through the box. He is a little dizzy and it doesn't help that everyone is punching his shoulder and smacking his helmet.

Johnny can hear his dad yelling from the stands, "Are you OK?" Johnny? Johnny gives the thumbs up.

The crowd roars as Kenny rips a side arm, low to high over the goalies shoulder from the left wing. Johnny bounces out to the X and prepares himself mentally. He blocks out everything and runs through a mental check list and is completely focused.

Johnny clamps and pulls it behind to Tommy. Tommy scoops, his wingman is all over him. He turns to rotate back to his left hand. The attackmen are swarming from the restraining line. Johnny breaks towards Tommy who tries to flip to Johnny, but he is hacked from behind by an attackman. The attackman quickly scoops and moves it to a middie that is pushing to the goal from the far side. They push the ball, its 3 on 2 and the middie draws the slide, looks to his left, and then comes back and feeds right to a wide open attackman, who slams it home. Billy had no shot; 3-1. This gets the Crusaders crowd fired up. Next goal: green! We're right back in it.

Johnny knows that they have controlled the game up until this point, but if Holy Family scores here they will be right back in it. He needs to get the ball and break their momentum. He quick clamps and rakes it to the side where he can get the ball himself. He scoops and races down the left side. The point quickly sets up in a left handed break as they see Johnny pushing to the goal with his stick in his left hand. He has half a step on his man and crosses the restraining line with no slide coming. Johnny gets to about 10 yards and lets it go, overhand bounce shot—just wide. Johnny gets wrecked by his defender. Vince backs it up and retains the ball.

Vince takes the ball at the end line. He cuts off a pick by Kenny at X. Kenny's defender jumps Vince and Kenny slips off to the left. Vince spins away from the double and pops to Kenny, who catches it over the shoulder righty, switches to his left hand, and sprints around the left side. Kenny fakes upper right and bounces it lower left around the goalie. Two man pick and roll to perfection. 4-1, the good guys.

The first period ends with both teams fighting for the ball off of the face off.

Coach P pulls everyone in and says, "Keep up the intensity and work the ball. It's all about defense, groundballs, being unselfish, and finishing your shots." Gentlemen I want to see hustle and smart play. Everyone bring it in. 1-2-3…" Everyone shouts, "BE THE BEST!"

Johnny trots out to the X. He is greeted by a 6'2" D man with a long pole. Everyone is shouting for "C Train" to "Eat him up! Your ball CTrain." He is glaring directly into Johnny's eyes. Johnny tries to look tough (all 5'5" and 112 lbs of him). He gives the D man the "yea right" look and gets ready for the face off. Johnny pops the ball out behind him to Tommy and goes to scoop, but the opposing wingman checks it away. The ball pops behind Tommy and the big D man scoops it in full stride. He barrels down the right side and draws a slide. The pole looks ready to let a rocket go, but at the last second he snaps a cross crease pass to a wide open attackman, who shoots off hip on Billy from the crease, 4-2. The Crusaders bench and fans erupt, "HERE WE GO CRUSADERS! RIGHT BACK IN IT! YOU'RE THE MAN! C-TRAIN, DO IT AGAIN!"

Johnny goes back to the face off X and gets ready to battle with C-Train.

They get down at the X. The ref blows the whistle. Johnny clamp rakes it to the side. Johnny scoops and runs through the ball. C-Train is all over him. The Holy Family coach is screaming for the defense to shutoff their man. The coach wants the Hills' defense to cover anyone that Johnny would pass to, so that C-Train can go 1on 1 with Johnny, hoping that he can strip Johnny or force him to make a bad pass. Johnny is running for his life; he is taking front checks across the gloves. C-Train back checks him and gets Johnny's shaft, but Johnny manages to hold onto the ball and sprints behind the cage with C-Train matching every step. Johnny has nowhere to go with it. Kenny tries to pop out, but his man is all over him. Kenny cuts backdoor on his man and gets a step. Johnny manages to slip him the ball. Kenny comes around the goal, but shoots it wide. Vince backs it up. Johnny trots off. He is trying to catch his breath and his heart is racing.

The Holy Family goalie snuffs a rocket from Kyle and hits his middie for a breakout pass. Holy Family has numbers 6 on 5; they push the ball. Everyone fills lanes. The middie with the ball drops it back to the trailer who has a lane down the right side. He fires a hard bounce shot that Billy deflects for a save. The ball bounces out in front of the goal where an attackman scoops and puts it behind Billy for a garbage goal. On the next face off C-Train catches Johnny off guard with a rake, scooping the ball and racing to the goal. He looks to fire a shot. Johnny tries to check his stick but just misses. The shot rockets to the top right corner, but Billy makes a huge save, screams break, and hits Tommy on an outlet. Johnny trots off and thinks, "Thank God for Billy." The half ends, 4-3.

Everyone is huddled at the corner of the field. Coach P is ticked because the team had dominated the game and they come into the half only up one goal and Holy Family has all the momentum. He barks, "GENTLEMEN, you are GIVING them the game. They think that they are going to take it. They think that you guys are NOTHIN! We have to stop turning the ball over and we need to finish our opportunities. Get a drink and decide what you guys are going to do in the second half."

Kenny tells Johnny, "Nice job on the face offs. Keep it up. We need it."

The teams get set for the second half. Johnny walks out to the face off X to find good old C-Train there waiting for him, chomping his mouth piece. The players get set and the ref places the ball and blows the whistle. Johnny clamps, pulls it behind him and sprints after it. Johnny scoops it when C-Train viciously hacks him across the right shoulder, sending Johnny flying. The ref calls a push from behind and awards the ball to the Hawks, but to the dismay of the Hawks fans, does not award a penalty.

The guys set up in a 1-4-1 with Vince receiving the ball up top. He drive stutters to his right and crosses over left, the defender is on him. Vince takes three more strong steps, plants, and rolls back right. The defensive slide is coming from the crease. Conor Malone has cut in from the right wing and Kenny has slipped behind him on the right side. Vince spots him and quickly feeds him. Kenny receives the ball wide open with no one on him. He sets his feet and lets an underhand low to high shot go. It's not even fair. The goalie drops to his knees as the ball whizzes over his shoulder near side high for a big goal.

Holy Family scores one in transition by pushing a 5 on 4 break. The goalie made a save and a nice outlet pass. After that they just outhustled the Hawks' middies into the hole. Coach P is livid that the middies get beat to the defensive end. He calls a time out.

The Hawks bring it in. "Gentlemen, the score is now 5-4 because we gave them a goal. Just gave it to them. They outhustled us, that is not what we are all about.

Second middies in, Jack you are in the box and you'll sub in for Johnny off the face. It's up to you gentlemen. Do you want it? 1-2-3…" "BE THE BEST!"

Johnny gets ready for the face off. Down, set, whistle. He clamps and pulls the ball to the side, scoops it and is off to the goal. He glances to the point, the slide isn't really coming. He gets to the restraining line and the D man starts to come over, but is cheating to the point. Johnny fakes a pass to point with his shoulders. The slide immediately hesitates and Johnny turns on the burners down the alley. When he gets to 10 yards, he rips an overhand bouncer at the goalie's feet to the far pipe. The shot beats the goalie and kisses off the pipe about 10 inches from the ground and into the net. The crowd erupts.

Johnny pulls the next face off back to Kyle, who runs it into the offensive end as Johnny trots through the box. Everyone is smacking him on the helmet and shoulder pad. Johnny hears his father screaming over the crowd, "Great shot, Johnny! All day on the X! All day!"

Back on the field, Kenny beats his man from the left wing, draws the slide, and hits Smitty who cuts perfectly behind the slide. He one-times it over the goalie's shoulder, 7-4. Johnny jogs out to the X and finds a long pole waiting for him. He knows that the pole is going to try to tie him up and will probably chop check on the whistle. He decides to push it forward with a rake where he will drop his stick backwards and push under the opponent's stick. DOWN, SET, WHISTLE!

Johnny is right. He pops the ball forward but stumbles out of his stance as the pole rams his shoulder into his hip. He gets to the ball just ahead of the crashing wing and is laid out. The ball goes flying. The long pole scoops it and charges downfield. He looks, shoulder fakes a pass to the point, and jets down the right handed fires a shot high to high, Billy starts to drop down low but catches himself and lunges back up to get his stick on the ball and deflect it over the goal. Johnny knows that he can expect the pole and pressure for the entire second half.

On the bench there is a feeling that they controlled the first half and the start of the 3rd and the Hawks should be up by more than 7-4. Kyle barks, "But we should be blowing these guys out. We should be up by six right now. We're only up by three and they are going to come out in the fourth quarter like gang busters. We've got to go out there and put 'em down. Take the game. FINISH THE JOB!"

Coach P walks in, the team huddle goes silent as everyone waits for him to speak. "Guys, this game is ours for the taking, are we going to take it? Or are we going to let them back in the game? We have to win the groundball battle. THEY WILL PRESSURE US! We have to HANDLE their pressure and stay aggressive. We also have to finish our opportunities. Let's go out as a team and everyone collectively, TAKE THIS GAME! It's our game IF we outwork them!"

The half begins with Johnny at the X with the long pole #42 snorting and glaring at him. Johnny clamps and pulls it between his legs. He gets it by himself. The attackman charges him from out of the box and the long pole is right on his tail and hacking him like a lumberjack trying to take down a redwood. He manages to push a pass to Billy in the goal, just before the charging attackman rams his shoulder into his gut. The ball bounces twice before Billy races to scoop it. The Hawks manage to clear. The ball gets worked around until Kenny slips behind his man and gets a quick feed, which he converts off the goalies hip. Kenny's father has ingrained in him that as soon as his defender turns his head to see the ball or help, you cut backdoor; if his head is on a swivel then you time the swivel. Kenny has turned this into an art and he has feasted off it for years. 8-4, good guys.

At the beginning of the 4th quarter the Hawks defense fights off multiple shots on a long Holy Family possession. RJ makes a great scoop on a groundball in traffic. He busts out and heads for the midline near the box. He is cut off by a middie and a riding attackman; he turns and fires it to an attackman near midfield. The pass floats a little and is intercepted by C-Train in full stride with his long pole. He sprints down the right side and rips a shot low to high, right over Billy's head. 8-5. The Holy Family bench and crowd explode. It's 8-5 Hawks, but Holy Family has all the momentum.

Johnny realizes that this face off is huge. He needs to stop the Holy Family run and gain possession for the Hawks. He approaches the X and C-Train is there waiting. The ref calls down and the two get set. He places the ball, backs up, and calls, "Down, Set" and blows the whistle. Johnny clamps and pulls the ball behind him. C-Train nearly runs him over from behind. Johnny stumbles but doesn't fall. He bursts after the ball with C-Train breathing down his neck and the defensive wing focusing in on Johnny. Johnny takes a step and runs up field. He scoops one handed with his left, plants his right foot, and shovels the ball up over his right shoulder as he is slashed by C-Train and laid out by the wingman. The ball lofts up in the air about 15 to 20 ft. right to RJ who has to stop and wait for it, but is so wide open that it doesn't matter. The ref throws his flag and his hat. RJ sprints downfield on a fast break. He hits Terry at the point and Terry fires it across to Mikey G., who rips it past the Crusader's goaltender. The ref signals goal and then calls C-Train and his wingman for a slash and a high hit. It's 9-5 and the Hawks will be up two men for a minute due to the penalties.

Johnny sprints over to the coach. He is feeling pretty woozy, but he tells Coach P to put one of the man-up middies on the wing because Holy Family will have an attackman on the wing that will not be able to cross midfield due to the penalties.

Coach puts Kyle on the wing and tells both Johnny and Kyle to get the ball. The ref blows the whistle. Johnny clamps and pulls the ball forward. It is an easy ground ball for Kyle because the attackman can only watch, as he has to stay on the sides. Johnny runs out through the box and the Hawks run their man up play. It's a 3-3 with a classic sneak around.

The score is 10-5 with five minutes left in the game. Johnny goes out for the face. He now has 2 offensive middies back and pulls it back to Jack Kelly. He scoops and is double teamed. LP #42 strips him and gets it to his attack. They work the ball around and get the offensive middies in the game. They run two man games up top, as well as behind the goal. They are peppering the net with rockets. Billy turns several shots and finally gets possession. They set up the clear and Billy moves it left to Smitty. He then redirects to Billy, who sends it over to the right. He is pressured between a box and midfield. He forces a pass to a middie in the middle of the field. It is picked off by a defensive middie, who pushes it to a streaking attackmen. They have a 2 on 1. The attackman draws the slide, hits the other attackman, and he bounces a lefty shot at Billy's feet. Billy gets a piece of it, but it scores anyway; 10-6, 3:40 left on the clock.

Next face off. Johnny pulls it behind and keeps it himself. The defense is screaming, "SHUT OFF" and good old Long Pole is all over him. Johnny is running for his life. He gets it over midfield and is running down the right side. The attack is breaking out, but they are covered. Johnny has a step and Long Pole is hacking. He slashes Johnny right across the back. Johnny goes flying and the ball goes out of bounds. The ref calls the penalty and the Hawks are a man up.

Coach P instructs the man up team to take about 40 seconds off the clock before they run the play, which they do, running a 3-3 man up offensive set. The ball works right and then back left. Smitty skips a pass down to Kenny in the bottom right handed spot. Kenny shoots it wide. 10-6, 2:20 left in the game. The Crusaders backup the goal and gain possession. They clear the ball and get it behind. Their attackman dodges and fires a shot. It's just wide, but the Crusaders maintain possession. They continue to pepper the goal and finally put one in with 55 seconds left.

Johnny is ready for the rake; he slides his stick down the line and clamps. This closes the lane and C Train is actually raking into his stick. (When Johnny pushes his left hand forward like normal, it opens the lane for a rake.) The change in strategy works like a charm. Johnny pulls it out to Jack Kelly. Jack runs the ball behind the goal and gets it to the attack; they have to keep it in the box. Kenny sprints back and forth on the end line. The Crusaders pull the goalie out of the crease and double the ball. Kenny moves the ball to Nick who then rotates it up top. Coach P screams to get it behind, everyone is shut off. Aidan sprints it behind the cage. He is doubled. He rolls the ball to X where there is wild fight for the ball. Kenny picks it up, but is checked immediately and the ball exits the box. Since you must keep it in the box in the last 2 minutes, it's a turnover. 17 seconds left. The Crusaders clear it with a middie running right to the goal. He cranks a shot but

Smitty is on his gloves. It is an easy save for Billy.The ball rebounds in front of the goal and the Crusaders score a meaningless garbage goal with the seconds left in the game. No one gains possession of the next face off as time expires. A 10-7 win for the Hawks.

Kenny and Johnny are finally dressed and leaving the locker room. Coach P walks with them saying, "First game under your belts, boys. Both of you did a great job, today. You hustled, played unselfishly and with composure. Johnny, your face offs were 16 for 19. Kenny you finished your shots. How many did you have, 3?"

Johnny says, "No, he had 4. He finished 'em all except for the one I fed him."

They all laughed.

Coach P, "Seriously, keep up the good work."

Johnny walked in the front door and finds his parents waiting for him.

Dad jumps out of his chair and says, "Nice game son!"

Mom gives him a kiss and a hug and says, "Nice game. Are you okay?"

Johnny, "Yes."

Mom, "I was so worried when that kid hit you on the face off. Those guys are all so much bigger than you. I don't like it."

Johnny says, "Mom, IT AINT BALLET!"

They all laugh. Mom says, "I made your favorite: chicken parm and linguine for dinner tonight." She yells upstairs for the girls to come down to eat.

They sit down and Dad says, "Janet the JV won 8-5. Johnny had a great game."

Kim asks, "How many goals?"

Dad says, "None, but they wouldn't have won without him."

Kim looks at Johnny and says with as much sarcasm as she can, "Oh so they wouldn't have won without your goose egg right? Whateva! Do we have to have chicken parm after every game all year??"

Dad shoots her a glare and says to knock it off.

Johnny rolls his eyes. He expects it from Kim. In fact if she had complimented him, Johnny might have choked on his chicken parm.

He wolfs down his dinner and says, "I have to study. I've got a math test tomorrow." He heads up to his room.

He cracks open the math text book and starts studying. His mind keeps drifting to the game. He continually has to refocus. He falls asleep after about an hour with the book across his chest.

He wakes the next morning when hears his sister turn on the shower. He can't believe that he fell asleep, he still has to review several formulas and memorize when he should apply them. He jumps out of bed.

CHAPTER 10:
THE SANDBOX

Johnny and Kenny are walking across the fields on their way home after practice and it is actually light out, as the clocks have sprung forward for daylight savings. The first Friday night of daylight savings is always the first practice for kids in the youth clinic. The six fields at Harborview High are teaming with players. Johnny and Kenny remember stories from when they were out there as 4 year olds. The action is fast, dust is flying, and parents are yelling "Get your back hand down when you scoop," "Put the stick in your other hand!" "Slide with the body!" and "GO TO THE GOAL!" When Phil Mooney misses an easy goal his father jokes that there will be no dinner for him. Everyone laughs but in reality, the sport is taken very seriously by coaches, parents, and the players. Many of the parents played for this P.A.L. program and for Harborview High School before heading off to play in college. They can't wait to see their kids play Port in the always intense rivalry game. The parents that didn't play are getting their kids into the game in hopes that it will get their child into a great college. If this sounds like alot of pressure, it's not because these kids are too young to know what pressure is. The six fields are filled by kids between Kindergarten and 2nd grade, and in the corner of the field is an age group called the "Mighty Mites" made up of four year olds and one kid that is three years old that actually shows up for practice in a pull-up diaper under his shorts. It seems that every year they start them younger. These guys are too young to learn the rules, so the play "wild man rules" meaning no boundaries and whoever scoops the ball, goes to the goal as all fourteen of the other players try to stop him. It is the lacrosse version of kill the guy with the ball. The kids love it! They play for forty-five minutes and then they go and play in the sand pit by the track and play with their trucks while their parents hit their coolers and kick off the weekend with a few cold ones. Just another Friday night around here.

The JV and Varsity finish a spirited practice. Everyone is pumped and works hard during sprints. The two teams are perfect so far with the JV going 4-0 and the varsity is 5-0. Coach P reminds the two teams that the heart of the schedule is coming up. Reminds them that NO ONE can get COMPLACENT! Their seasons are going to come down to how BADLY THEY WANT TO WIN! and the AMOUNT OF WORK that they are WILLING TO PUT INTO THE SEASON! We need to get better today, tomorrow and EVERY DAY from here on out! Face off guys at the X, everyone else can hit the showers.

The guys know the routine…you win you stay in. You lose, to the end of the line. Johnny has been getting the best of everyone recently and is out there first. He beats Kyle then Robby and Zach. Then he beats Ryan. At Coach Sipp's suggestion, Coach P has stuck around to watch the face off work. Johnny has won seven in a row on clamps, pulling the ball to the side and behind him and winning them cleanly, Coach P barks "Doesn't anyone want to beat this 8th grader? He is owning you guys." Johnny wins 9 or 10 more in a row. Finally Tyler Simmons jumps the whistle and wins. Coach P laughs, but lets it go. Ryan quickly beats Tyler, then Kyle and Robby. Coach P blows the whistle and tells them to hit the showers. As the face off guys jog off Coach P yells for Johnny to hold up. He walks with Johnny and tells him that if he wants to work, really work hard that he has the chance to be a special face off man and maybe a very good all around player as well. Pound the books and if you are willing to REALLY WORK you can be special here and you'll have the college coaches knocking down your door.

Johnny says "Thanks coach. I work on face offs all the time and my stick work too." Coach says, "That's great! Pushing on the books is what it's all about though." Johnny replies "Will do coach, thank you." Then Coach asks," if he is ready for the big game against the hated Port Jeff Patriots." Johnny replies, Coach, I have been waiting for this for as long as I can remember. I will be ready." Coach just grins.

A few captured moments of some of the inspirations for this book

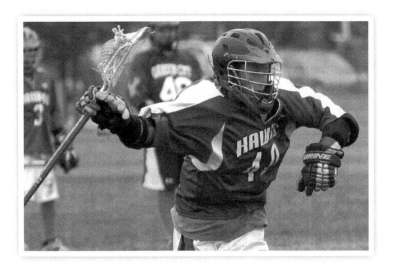

CHAPTER II:
THE PORT GAME

The team exits the locker room with shouts and whoops that echo in the short tunnel that leads to the field. Some of the varsity guys bump knuckles as the players pass through. Johnny passes Ryan who pounds him on the shoulder and yells, "Your day Johnny, be the man. The ball is yours ALL DAY!"

The guys head through the tunnel. Their shouts echoing in the narrow tunnel: "OUR FIELD, BABY! OUR DAY! BLUE n WHITE EVERYWHERE! ALL DAY BABY! ALL DAY! The Hawks take a lap around the field and there is a burst of applause as they pass the home stands, which are more crowded than usual and filling up. The game is 45 minutes away. Johnny is super stoked as the Port game is the most intense rivalry game that he has ever played in.

Warm-ups fly by as the whole team is buzzing. Billy looks sharp in the net as always, the face off guys pair off and get some quick work in. The Dmen bang shoulders. Coach P calls everyone in and says, "Gentlemen this is what we've been waiting for, what we've been working for. Nothing needs to be said. We're ready, I can see it in your eyes." These two teams have been going at it since the beginning of PAL lacrosse, but now the stakes are raised.

Coach P pulls the squad in for last minute instructions. He goes over the starting attack and defense. He says, "Johnny you've got the face. Kyle you've got a wing, Jake you're on the defensive wing with the pole. We'll have Sully in the box, ten man ride, we'll get a pole near the box on the clear so we can sub in a shortie if we want. Billy SHUT THE DOOR! All hands in. 1-2-3." The whole squad shouts, " BE THE BEST!"

The teams line up while the refs give instructions, the goalies shake hands then everyone else does.

The teams are set, the crowd has three or four hundred, and people are streaming in. There is a lot of yelling "Let's go Blue! You da man Billy!" "You're ball Johnny!" (Johnny recognizes his father's voice).

The ref places the ball and shouts, "Down!, Set!" and blows the whistle. Johnny gets a quick clamp and pulls it to the side, he grabs the ball and is hit by the defending wingman, but Johnny manages to flip it over the defender's shoulder. It bounces twice and Kyle scoops it easily. Johnny heads for the box, totally fired up. The Hawks settle the ball, move it around, everyone getting a touch.

Kenny split dodges and lets a left handed rip go in the alley. The ball rebounds off the goalie's shoulder. Nick McInnis is in the right place and scoops it and puts it over the goalies shoulder for a garbage goal and 1-0 lead.

Johnny pushes the next draw out in front and has a step for a break. He pushes the ball and draws the slide. Johnny hits the point, over to Kenny, Kenny pops it to Aidan for an easy goal.... Two nil good guys. On the next face off, Kyle runs over the ball and Port is able to gain possession. Tre Johnson, the youngest of four brothers to play at Port, demands the ball on the right wing. He split dodges right to left and streaks in along the goal line extended. He gains a step on Tommy Smith and he dives in front of the goal just before he reaches the crease and is able to reach around Billy and gets a shot off just before he is leveled by Cade. Johnson winds up in the crease, but the goal stands as the ref rules that he was pushed into the crease. The Port fans erupt in applause.

Johnny heads out for the next draw knowing that he can quickly put an end to the Port momentum by winning the face. He wins the clamp cleanly and pulls it back between his legs. He sprints for the ball and bends to scoop. The face off man lifts his bottom hand and Johnny runs over the ball. The Patriots jump all over the loose ball. They work it up top in a 1-4-1. Billy yells to the D, "Woody you're hot, you go." The middie split dodges left. The left wing cuts through and as Woody slides the crease men run a mumbo pick and cut underneath and the crease middie pops open about six yards on the left wing. He catches the ball, turns and fires G money. Billy makes a tremendous off hip save that fires up the entire squad. The Hawks are able to clear the ball and settle it behind the goal in their offensive end. Kenny receives the ball behind the goal and drives around the right side. He hits Aidan Quinn 3 yards off the crease with a beautiful no look pass. Aidan bounces it inside the right pipe for a 3-1 Hawks lead. Johnny is able to gain possession on the next face off and Nick McInnis notches his second goal of the day to give the Hawks a 4-1 lead. Everything is going in the Hawks favor until Port breaks a Hawks clear with a tremendous ride and effort from Tre Johnson. He strips Woody, pounces on the groundball and is off like a shot towards the goal. He draws a slide and moves it to a wide open attackman on the crease. Billy comes out of the crease and almost lays the Port attackman out, but the Port player manages to side step Billy at the last minute and is able to shoot into the empty net just before the 1st quarter ends. In the second quarter Kenny had 2 goals with one of them being a beautiful crank from the right wing that could not have been placed anymore in the upper right corner. Unfortunately Tre Johnson would answer with 2 goals of his own and the squads would go into the half with a score of 6-4 favoring the Hawks.

Everyone takes a knee, grabs a water bottle and huddles around Coach P. Coach tells the squad that they are letting Port hang around when they should be putting the game away. The Hawks have controlled the ball most of the game, but have gotten sloppy at times. He makes adjustments and decides to have Cade deny the ball to Tre Johnson. He tells the team to be prepared to slide early should Johnson get a step on Cade. He tells the Offense to watch the sloppy passes, not to force it to the crease and to finish their shots. He concludes by saying, "Gentlemen, this game is there for the taking. Are we going to take it? ARE WE GOING TO TAKE IT!?"

Johnny lines up for the draw and is totally focused. He is able to clamp the ball and push it in front of him for a fast break. He scoops the ball on a dead run, draws the slide and hits Nick on the point, Nick moves it to Kenny. Kenny sees an opening and fires overhand to the lower right corner. There are a few shouts of Brocho Cinco! The Hawks score the first goal of the second half in 9 seconds. The Hawks convert two more face off wins by Johnny into goals and the Hawks have extended the lead to 9-4 . On the other end of the field Cade has shut off Tre Johnson and Port has struggled to score. Port finally manages to score with about 40 seconds left in the 3rd quarter and the score is 9-5, which is how the period ends.

The home crowd is on their feet cheering on the Hawks as the 4th quarter begins. Johnny digs his feet in and readies for the face off. His opponent from Port jumps the whistle and gets away with it. He pulls the ball back behind him and chases it to scoop it. Jake flies in off the wing and lays out the Port middie with a crushing hit. He is a little over zealous and follows through on the hit with his stick and gets called for cross checking. Port quickly takes advantage of the man up opportunity as Tre Johnson rifles a shot in from top right in a 3-3 set. 9-6 Hawks.

Johnny pulls the ball to himself on the next draw, but has it checked away just as he scoops it. The Port crowd and bench come to life as as a Port long pole sprints through the pile of players, scoops the ball on the run and heads right for the goal. Cade is forced to slide to the long pole and Tre Johnson sneaks around the crease where he catches a feed from the long pole and is able to dip and dunk to make the score 9-7. The Hawks extend the lead to 3 only to have Port respond right away and make it a 2 goal game with 2:20 left on the clock. Johnny knows that he has to have the next face off. He pulls it out to Jake who scoops it and lofts a pass to Aidan, but the pass floats a little too much and is knocked to the ground. Johnny is on his way to the substitution box when out of the corner of his eye, he sees that the ball is on the ground about 5 yards outside the restraining line. He turns and sprints to the ball, scoops it and runs four steps inside the box. He lets an overhand bounce shot go. Johnny is knocked to the ground just as he releases the shot and he never sees the ball hit the top left corner. The home crowd goes nuts as it will be tough for Port to overcome a 3 goal lead with 1:52 left on the clock. When Johnny wins the next face off a comeback is even more improbable. Kenny, Aidan and Vince kill the clock and the crowd counts down the last ten seconds. The clock expires and the Hawks sprint to Billy in goal.

The locker room is jubilant and very boisterous as everyone is super pumped about the victory. Coach P tells the team that he loves the way they played, especially in the second half. He tells the team to enjoy the win, go cheer on the varsity team, no booze, carousing or funny business, enjoy it, but to make sure they will be there at 9 a.m. The entire team groans, "PRACTICE at NINE". Coach says, "We could make it 8 and if I smell so much as a beer on anyone, you won't be needing your sticks." The players know by that he means that they will be running the entire practice. Everyone showers quickly as the varsity is about to start. Tommy Smith is busy primping in the mirror as Kenny and Johnny stroll by. "FLOW boys, the ladies love it! By the way, you punks played pretty well. Nice job. No wedgies for a while. See you out there. Tell the girls not to worry, T will be there soon."

Mr. Artuso, the trainer, grabs Johnny and says, "You've got to ice that shoulder. I'll wrap it on with an ace bandage. We'll get you out there quickly." He wraps a bag of ice over Johnny's tee shirt with an ace bandage. Kenny and Johnny are so freaking happy that they don't care if they ever leave the locker room, but they finally do. They are the last to leave the locker room as usual. They climb the stairs slowly both stiff, sore, and exhausted. It feels great. They pass Coach P at the exit. He is enjoying himself and talking to a few parents. He is beaming and says, "Gentlemen, congratulations you played great, not perfect but we got it done against these guys. Go cheer on the varsity. I will see you guys at 9 tomorrow."

The boys weave through the cluster of players, getting knuckles from their teammates and pats on the back from parents. "Way to fill it up Kenny and great job at the X Johnny! Great having you guys on the team." The boys can not believe the buzz and how pumped everyone is. The feeling is magical and better than they ever imagined, which is saying alot.

They locate their parents and Kenny's dad comes up and throws his arms around both of them and says, "I am so proud of both of you guys!" Johnny grunts as Mr. K is crushing his shoulder. He quickly apologizes.

The smile on Janet's face quickly slumps to a look of worried concern. She approaches firing questions, "What happened? Are you okay? We should get this looked at. Carl what do you think? Johnny, are you okay?"

Johnny replies, "Mom, I'm fine. It's just a bruise, I need to ice it and to get new shoulder pads."

His mom says, "Rob, you are going to get him new pads tomorrow, right?"

Carl replies, "Of course. First thing, how's my man? That was some game you guys played. How about that? How'd it feel to throw in that fourth goal? Kenny, the backbreaker, how'd it feel?"

Everyone laughed as Kenny blushed, rolled his shoulders and turned his palms up and said, "You know" as he shined his nails on his chest.

Someone screamed "Yeah baby!" BROCHO CINCO you THE MAN!"

They all laughed gave knuckles and slapped five until someone asked if anyone knew the varsity score. Johnny and Kenny said they were going to catch up with their friends over at the field. His parents said they would be watching it with Kenny's parents and the Healy's on the stands on the far side. Johnny's mom told them to "Have fun but be home by 10:30." Kenny and Johnny headed to the hill at the south end of the field to catch up with the crew. Kenny said "That's where everyone is hanging as usual."

Johnny turned on his phone and there were several messages.

RJ—Great game!

Allie—Nice! Sweet win! Are you ok?

Shane—Way to bury the Patriots. They got the beating that they deserved

Alley—See you at the game!

Shane—Varsity game is about to start. Move it!

The boys are walking the couple hundred yards to the field. It is packed, more than they remembered last year's games being. Every parking spot is filled. They lights are on as it is just getting dark.

They find the crew dead center of the hill. Nick, Knarles, Kim, Janet, Allie, Kelly, Vince, and Matt! Temperature in the 70's. Things are looking and feeling good. They exchange knuckles with all the guys, say hello to the girls and grab a seat with the crew. The score is now 3-2 the good guys. Nick says, "That Ryan ripped a side arm rocket, upper right and had a sweet split dodge for a feed that set up a goal. No assist, but a hockey assist. He made the whole thing happen."

The Patriots score to make it 3-3. Jeremy tells Johnny that Ryan beat his man and fed for an assist on the first goal and ripped rocket upper right for the second. The two face off men get tied up for about 15 seconds. Finally Ryan manages to push Ainge off the ball, but there is no clear advantage as both teams players are on top of the ball. There is a huge hack fest until a Patriot's pole finally grabs it. The pole gets the ball to the attackman on the wing, it goes to X and the attack man drives the right hand side and finds a middie cutting down the left side, score tied at 3. The team exchange goals and it is four all, until Ryan split dodges left and bounces a rocket off hip on the right pipe for a 5-4 halftime lead.

Johnny says to Kenny, "Check out this crowd. Talk about nuts!" It must be 4,000 easy. Kenny replies, "How many people were at the varsity baseball game…50-60? Nothing but parents and three or four girlfriends. Same crowd kindergarten through high school." The two crack up laughing.

Johnny says Ryan is having some game, 3 and an assist in the first half.

Kenny replies, "We're going to play in this. Maybe next year."

Johnny says, "Bro, you keep it up and you'll be called up for the playoffs."

Kenny, "Yea right, not way."

Johnny, "No way? Try NO FREAKIN DOUBT ABOUT IT."

R.J. swings around the field with Brian and J.P. They exchange knuckles and low fives. The guys say great job in the game to Kenny and Johnny. Brian says, "How many did you have Kenny?" Johnny says, "He had four and two." Brian responds "Hey that's four and two more than you, Johnny, psyche!"

Kenny says "Actually Johnny scored a huge goal and owned the X all day. Where were you in the can?"

Allie jumps in, "No, he was just too busy being jealous, and muttering to himself that he belongs on the JV. PSYCHE!"

Everyone Cracks up as Brian barks "SHUT UP Alley!" then he motions to Johnny and says, "You'll never be more than a FOGO anyway." He storms off.

R.J. says "Johnny, don't worry about him."

Johnny responds, "No worries he's cool. He just works so hard and wants it so bad. He'll be fine."

Timmy says, "No worries? Damn straight no worries my man just owned the X and scored the goal that put the dagger in the freaking Patriots, now he's on the hill watching the Varsity all snuggled up with his girl Allie. No worries? You can't beat the smile off his face with a baseball bat! Uh Uh Huh!" They all howl.

The crowd explodes as the team re-enters the field and begins to warm-up. Tunes cranking, huge crowd. What a night! The coaches finish warming up the goalies and all the players bring it in for last minute instructions from the coaches. The Hawks hang all their hands in "1-2-3 Be the Best!"

Ryan walks to the face off X and Johnny yells, "Let's go Rhino , you own him. Your ball Rhino!"

The ref places the ball, yells "Down, Set" whistle. Ryan tries to rake it, but Ainge clamps it and pulls it out cleanly to his wing. The Port long pole scoops it, but is jumped by Jack McInnis who quickly strips him and heads to the Hawks offensive end, runs it in and dumps it to the attackman on the right wing. They get it to X and sub on the fly. The ball works around the horn and gets to Ryan up top. Jack cuts through. Ryan split dodges left to right and has a step and a half on his man. The slide is there as the Patriots are sliding to Ryan early. Ryan spins back left and hits Vince who catches it right handed and hops twice to shoot. The second slide stops and braces for the shot, but Vince face dodges, switching to his left for a running bouncer that beats the purple goalie off hip. The crowd erupts 7-4.

Next face off: Ainge wins the draw and gets it himself. He runs it into the offensive end. The ball works to the right wing then behind to X. The attack men drives the opposite side, Ainge cuts off a high double pick and receives a ball left handed and zips a bouncer off hip. Dano somehow deflects it wide. The Patriots maintain possession and their attackman drives from the wing. He takes Teddy Smith high and slips underneath him and Smitty back checks the Port attackman and helicopters his stick. Smitty scoops the ball and heads up field, but Port strips Smitty on the ride at midfield and they push it ahead to a cutting attack man. It is a race to the goal, 3 on 2 the attack man cuts to his left about ten yards from the crease, drawing a man and pulling the other defensemen to attackman on the left. He lobs it over the defenseman to the attack man on the right. He catches it lefty, fakes lower left and fires it lower right for a goal 7-5. The Port crowd comes to life with a roar.

Kenny says, "That's not good. My dad always tells me that a game can change on a ride. He's been telling me since I was six. You want to ride like some legendary guy, Mike O'Neil. He played against him in high school when they played Massapequa. They played together at Hopkins. I've heard about him fifty times a week since we've been playing…Mike O'Neil, Mike O'Neil, Mike O'Neil," Kenny imitates his father's gestures. The whole group has played for Kenny's father since they were six. They howl with laughter as they know the Mike O'Neil speech and Kenny does a good job of mimicking his father. Johnny adds, "But we WERE the best riding team on the island all through PAL" he puts his hand out and the boys give knuckles all around.

Ryan and Ainge get set for the face off, the ref blows the whistle. Ainge clamps it between his legs and scoops it, runs it to the box and gets it to the righty attackman on the wing. Port works the ball behind where the attackman dodges and uses a finalizer move to get a step on his man on the left side. He cuts to goal line extended and fakes a pass to the crease, the slide hesitates on the fake and the attackman takes two more steps and shoots it around Dano, 7-6. Dano tells Charlie if you're going to go, you GOTTA PUT HIM ON HIS BACK! You can't go halfway.

The crowd is roaring and on their feet as they fourth quarter is set to begin. No one seems to notice that it has begun to rain. Ainge pops the ball out in front of him. Ryan is on his heels and Vince checks Ainge's stick, the ball pops further forward to the Hawk's defensive end where it is scooped by the pole from Port. The ref calls release as soon as it is scooped, Charlie releases from the defensive box and lays out the pole with a monster hit with the ferociousness of a middle linebacker. The crowd goes berserk, as the teams scramble for the loose ball. It goes out of bounds off of Port. Hawk's ball. The tone has been set for the rest of the game. It is going to be a dog fight.

The Hawks get off three pretty good shots but are denied when the Port goalie controls it on a save and hits a breaking middie on a clear. It's a 5 on 4 and they push it. They make three quick passes and the Port lefty sniper buries one from six yards out, 7-7.

Ainge goes forward with it and has a step. He bursts right down the right alley and pulls his stick back but then tucks it as Ryan attempts a check at it. He then fires one upper left, 8-7, the bad guys. Coach Martin calls for a time out. The home crowd is anxious as all the momentum has shifted to Port.

On the face off, Jack Mcinnis is lined up at the top of the wing to guard against a fast break. The whistle blows, Ainge pulls the ball back to his unguarded wing man. Port controls the ball with 5:49 seconds left on the clock. They run it around the horn twice and start to attack. Ainge split dodges up top in a 1-4-1. He shoots it wide but the Patriots retain it. They give it to Ainge again. He dodges right, rolls back left as the right wing man cuts through and the crease men pick and mumbo cut. The d slides and Ainge hits the crease men on the right side for a four yard shot, 9-7 with 3:47 left on the clock.

On the next faceoff Ryan guesses that Ainge will clamp with Jack taking away the fast break. He decides to chop check over the ball and he gets his thumb under the corner of Ainge's stick and pushed him off the ball. Ryan scoops it and is pushed from behind by a furious Ainge. Hawks go man up for 30 seconds.

No time out is necessary. The Hawks go to a 3-3. The ball rotates left and back around to lower right. Reds skips to Ryan top middle and he rips a side arm crank that drills the pipe about an inch below the cross bar and into the net. The home crowd is ecstatic. 2:50 on the clock.

Johnny is yelling, "C'mon Ryan we need the ball. You get the ball and we got em." Alley sees that Johnny is as keyed up as if were playing. She strokes his back and grabs his hand. When Johnny finally realizes Allie is holding his hand he pulls it up to his face, gives her a kiss and a huge smile. She says, "They need you out there." Johnny shrugs his shoulder and laughs.

On the ensuing faceoff Ainge is ready for the chop and beats him with a "clam rake", which is quick half clamp that is quickly pulled to the side. Ainge grabs it himself and starts for the box.

Ryan just misses on a one handed over the head check, Ainge settles it up top and they move it behind. Coach Martin is yelling to "step out the d" and "shut off the adjacent pass." The clock runs down to 2:00 and the ref yells to "keep it in the box." The Port attack runs the ball back and forth on the end line. They set picks for each other. Smitty doubles off of one of the picks and dislodges the ball but a flag is thrown. Port goes man up for one minute with 1:19 to go. They work the ball and run the clock down to 38 second. They go 3-3- into a 1-3-2, they rotate and replace. They run the sneak and get it back down to the trailer and put one in for a 10-8 lead with twenty-four seconds left.

Ainge clamps and pulls it to himself, he sprints down the sideline" and behind the goal. An attackman picks and rolls and Ainge flips it to him as he gets doubled, the goalie covers the crease man and the crease defenseman goes to cover the ball. The attack man sprints to the back corner of the box as the Port crowd begins the ten second count down. He rolls it to the far corner of the box. It rolls out of the box with four ticks left. Smitty picks the ball up. When the ref blows the whistle, Smitty heaves it for the crease. It's knocked away. The Patriots pile on their goalie in celebration. The home crowd and home team are both stunned and stung by the defeat.

CHAPTER 12:
INJURED

Johnny was awakened by the searing pain from the huge black and blue bruise on his shoulder. He was very stiff as he hobbled downstairs and threw a bag of ice on the shoulder. He popped a pair of pop tarts in the toaster and sat down with some O.J. He noticed it was 5:45am, the earliest he had ever been up at on a Saturday. Johnny's mom heard him banging around the kitchen and grimaced when she saw the bag of ice, "How's the shoulder?"

Johnny rolled his eyes and said, "Fine."

She walked up from behind him, grabbed the ice pack and pulled the shirt from the neck. Johnny pulled away and grabbed his collar but it was too late. He knew that Janet Price had seen the deep purple bruise by the way she sighed.

Johnny said, "Mom it's not ballet, I'm fine."

His mother replied, "Very funny mister and not only are you not fine, but you are NOT PLAYING until you see a doctor."

Johnny sharply retorts, "I AM PLAYING, I AM NOT MISSING A PRACTICE!"

Dad is standing at the kitchen door and says, "What's up?"

Janet says, "Look at his shoulder, I told you that these kids were too big. He needs to see a doctor."

Carl takes a look at his shoulder saying, "I'll call Dr. Fuentes. He was at the game last night and I bet he will see you sometime today. We'll call him around 9."

The next two hours seemed like weeks. Johnny was up and down the stairs and extremely restless. He was upstairs in his room practicing shops and quick clamps while listening to random whistles on his iPod?

His mother came up to get him. She is yelling at him. Johnny can't hear her because he is so focused and has earphones in. Kim is screaming at him at him, "Shut up you loser, it isn't even eight o'clock in the morning!" Look at you, headphones on to random whistles. She gives him the big L on the far head. Janet says, "Kim knock it off! And you might want to keep it down as well! Ryan is downstairs." Johnny and mom see Kim's eyes light up when she hears that Ryan is sitting on the couch. She is visibly disappointed when she finds out that he is waiting for Johnny.

Johnny pops downstairs and gives Ryan some knuckles. Johnny says, "Tough one bro, you had some great rips."

Ryan replies, "not enough and I couldn't win a faceoff to save my life. We have some work to do, bro. I saw the lights on and figured I would come over."

Johnny says, "Cool. Let's get started."

They go out back with their sticks. Johnny's got the random whistles on the iPod. They take turns practicing quick clamps. Ryan asks about his shoulder. Johnny tells him the deal and how they are waiting to call Dr. Fuentes.

Ryan says, "Good luck bro. Get well. We may need you come playoffs."

Johnny laughs and says, "Don't let my mom hear that." They both laugh.

Johnny says, "You'll be able to handle Ainge next time."

They practice quick clamps some more, then some chops and a few rakes. After about forty minutes, Janet yells out to them that she has bacon and eggs if they want it. Ryan looks at Johnny and says, "Brother, that sounds awesome. Let's hit it." They head into the kitchen and there is Kim, ridiculously decked out and made up. She innocently says, "Ryan I didn't know you were still here?" Johnny just rolls his eyes and snickers.

Ryan replies, "Your little bro is helping me out on faceoffs."

Kim laughs and says, " You mean that YOU are helping HIM."

Ryan replies, "No, he is helping me. Your little brother's move is incredible. If I could've won a few face offs in the second half last night, we would've won the game."

Carl walks in to the kitchen and says that Dr. Fuentes has headed out east for the day and will not be able to see Johnny, but has arranged for Dr. Healy to see him. Dr. Healy makes time for Johnny and meets him in the office at 12 noon on Sunday. There aren't many doctors like him anymore. Dr. Healy asks Johnny about the JV game and tells him that he saw the Varsity, "Too bad we couldn't pull it out, but we'll seem them again and get another chance." Doc played and graduated in '82. they won the LI Championships and lost in the state finals to Yorktown 9-8. he asks Johnny to take off his shirt so he can have a look.

Johnny removes his shirt and the big purple bruise is immediately visible. Doc checks the range of motion asking, "Does this hurt? How about now? Now?"

He says, "You definitely have a pretty good bruise and you might have dislocated it and it popped right back in. I need you to get an MRI."

Johnny says, "Can I play?" Doctor Healy replies, "I want to see the MRI first. It's good that it's your left shoulder because the right would take a beating facing off, but we don't want to rush this. I know how much it means to you, right now it means everything, but we don't want to have a problem three years from now when you are on Varisty because we didn't take care of this properly now, right?"

Johnny can't even answer. He just sighs and looks at the ground.

Doc says, "Look we'll put you in a sling. I want you to ice it, we'll get an MRI tomorrow and we'll take a good look. We'll know more then."

Johnny says, "I was just facing off with Ryan this morning. NO PROBLEM! Not at all!"

Dr. Healy says, "Let's get the MRI, okay?"

Johnny's dad says, "You're the best doc. Thank you."

Johnny says, "Thank you for coming and seeing me."

Doc says, "See you tomorrow."

Dad calls mom on the phone and gives her the rundown. Tells her they are swinging by Di Ramo's to pickup lunch. They order two pies, some wings and Johnny's favorite chicken parm hero. Johnny texts Kenny and T.J. to come over to watch the UVA v Carolina game on ESPNU. When they get home Johnny gets comfortable on the couch with his chicken parm and wings and bag of ice on the shoulder. He grabs the remote and flips on the game.

The next day Johnny goes and gets an MRI. He is lucky that there are no tears and no breaks in the collar bone. He has a sprain and will miss two and a half weeks. In the time that Johnny is out the team wins three games, but lose their rematch to their rival the Port Patriots. Johnny was definitely missed in the loss as they struggled on face offs in the 11-9 defeat. Johnny can not wait to get back in the action and help the team. His first game back will be against the always tough Yorktown Huskers squad from Westchester.

CHAPTER 13:
YORKTOWN

The Hawks JV lines up for the Yorktown pre-game warm ups and Johnny is really excited as he stretches and does his pre game face off routine. He sees the Yorktown face off men practicing and notices that one of them is extremely thick. He is nervous as he normally gets butterflies in the stomach before a big game, but he is confident in his abilities as well. He is determined to get the best of his opponents and to help his team. The ref calls out the captains and Johnny notices that #44, the big guy that was facing off is one of the captains. He is built like a gorilla. The teams shake hands and get set for the opening draw.

Johnny hears his teammates and some parents screaming, "Your ball Johnny," "Get us started Johnny," "All day, kid you da man."

The ref places the ball and says, "Down, Set" and blows the whistle, Johnny clamps and has the edge, but has trouble getting the ball clamped enough to pull it out. It is as if he is trying to clamp against a brick wall. Johnny tries to rotate his body around the ball to gain leverage, but he gets pushed off the ball by the larger opponent, who manages to break away from the pack. Kyle is trying to beat him into the hole on the defensive end and is even with him until they reach the restraining line, where the big face off man hits an extra gear and gains a step down the alley. He rips an overhand right shot to the lower left corner and the Yorktown crowd erupts with a chant of, "Riggo! Riggo!" The Hawks aren't sure if Riggo is his name or his nickname as he is built like former NFL running back John Riggins and he sports a mohawk for a haircut.

Johnny manages to pull out the next draw and get it himself, but the Hawks offense gives up the ball on a turnover. The Huskers clear it and get it behind to a small shifty attackman (#22) who beats his man and forces the defense to slide. He hits a cutting middie and it's 2-0 Yorktown.

On the next face off, Johnny pulls it back cleanly, but is checked as he tries to scoop it. Yorktown gains another possession and settle in to their offense. They move the ball crisply and dodge in to the middle and cut out making a V shape to receive the passes. All of the passes are placed perfectly to the outside shoulder. The ball finally finds it's way to 22. He receives the ball at "X" behind the goal, dodges left, rolls back to his right only to use a quick finalizer move back to his left again. Tommy Smith has been staying right with him until the final move causes him to trip over the net. 22 scoots around the net, draws a slide and hits the crease attackman for a quick stick goal. It's 3 to zip and the Yorktown crowd is going nuts. The Hawks finally get a possession as Johnny pulls the draw back to Jake who gets it to Aidan on the wing. Aidan bumps it behind the goal to Nick who initially slips but manages to beat his man to the right side. He finds Kenny stepping in behind his man with a nice angle to the goal. Nick hits Kenny with a feed and Kenny let's go his patented low to high, side arm laser to the upper right corner. The Hawks are finally on board with just over two minutes left in the first quarter. Johnny has beaten Riggo pretty cleanly on the last two draws and Riggo has begun using a chop move to try and push Johnny off of the ball in hopes of making it a 50/50 scramble for a loose ball. The Huskers score two more goals and go up 5-1 with 25 seconds left in the half. Johnny tells his wingmen to box out their men to give Johnny a clean shot at the ball. Johnny correctly anticipates the chop move from Riggo. He counters this by dropping his stick backwards until it is parrallell to the ground, he then pushes the ball forward and under Riggo's stick. The ball shoots forward and Johnny scoops it on the run for a fast break. He hits Aidan at the point, he moves it to Kenny who quickly pops it over to Christain LeCompte, who finishes the break by putting it past the goalie with 16 seconds left on the clock. Johnny knows that Riggo is not chopping on the next one, so he clamps and pulls it back to Jake, who scoops it with a full head of steam. Jake heads right down the right alley with a step on his man. He draws a slide and manages to float a pass over the Husker defense to Kenny on the right wing. Kenny cranks a heater that blasts off the post right where the right pipe meets the cross bar. The ball shoots out to about 5 yards in front of the crease. There is a wild scrum of bodies fighting for the ball. Jake absolutely levels a Husker just as he picks up the ball. The hit is clean, but the ref throws the flag. It's Husker's possession with 3 seconds left in the half. They maintain possession until half and will begin the 3rd quarter with the ball and a man up opportunity.

At halftime Coach P is incensed. He barks, "Gentlemen, we are giving them the game! Every groundball comes up green! Turnovers all over the place. It's like we don't even WANT the ball! We dug ourselves a hole, who is going to step up!? Who is going to start making plays!? Who, gentlemen!? Who will, ANYONE?

The Hawks had some life at the end of the half, but the Huskers score on a sneak right at the end of their man up opportunity. The Hawks battle back as they get fired up by some big hits from Jake and Charlie. They get as close as a goal at 7-6, but Yorktown uses another man up situation to make it 8-6 on a hard shot from up top by Riggo in a 3-3 set. The Hawks do cut the lead to 8-7 on a hard bounce shot from Vince Collins, but that is all they could muster and the game ends 8-7 in favor of the bad guys. It's a game that the guys know that they should've won.

The bus ride home is quiet and brutal. Everyone on the team feels sick to their stomachs and to add insult to injury, there is a huge traffic jam. The traffic starts on the Hutchinson River Parkway, extends over the Throgs Neck Bridge and onto the Cross Island all the way to the L.I.E. The trip takes nearly three and a half hours.

When Johnny gets home, his dad says, "Tough one my man, but you did pretty well at the X, 10 of 18 and that Riggo kid was good, the best that you've seen all year. You almost had em."

Johnny just grunts in disgust. His mom makes him eat and he goes to bed, luckily it's a Friday and he doesn't have to do homework. He feels awful and he is wiped out.

CHAPTER 14:
THE PRACTICE

Practice is at 8 a.m. Saturday morning. Everyone is sore and tired from the Yorktown game and the team knows that Coach P will be ticked. They all expect the worst and their fears are soon confirmed when Coach sticks his head in the locker room door and says, "You won't be needing your sticks meet me on the track in two minutes." The guys head out through the tunnel and begin to stretch out on the track. Coach P tells the squad that they have six minutes to complete the mile and that for every player that does not make it under six minutes, there will be a full field suicide for the entire team. Everyone finishes in time except for big Bobby Curry who lumbers in at 6:22. His face is completely purple and no one gives him a hard time because they know that he tried his best and that 6:22 is the best time he has ever run.

Coach says, that the team has two minutes to walk it off and then to line up on him for 220 yard sprints. The guys are back on the line in what seems like 30 seconds. Coach methodically says, " Attack go." Tens seconds later he says, "Middies, go." Then "Defense."

The team proceeds to run endless amounts of 100 yarders then 40s as Coach screams at them, "They let Yorktown take it to them! How they were OUTHUSTLED! OUT WORKED! and how they showed NO HEART in the first half. Yes gentlemen, we did battle back in the 2nd half, but it was too late. There is no excuse for a lack of effort." He then yells, "Suicide for Mr. Curry not finishing on time. Everyone on the endline. Attack go! Middies go! D go!

Coach then says, "Great teams, teams with character, they respond to a loss. Dogs gentlemen, they roll over. What's it going to be gentlemen? It's up to you. Hit the showers."

Jake calls a players meeting in the locker room and informs the team that they only have four games left and he will not allow anyone to give less than 100% effort for even one second of any game or practice. He finishes the meeting by saying, "Everyone of you guys better go all out all the time or you will have to deal with me!"

Kenny looks to Johnny and says, "Wouldn't want to be on his bad side." Johnny just nods in agreement.

The team really responds to Coach P and Jake and the next three practices are at break neck pace. In their first game after Yorktown they pound Middle Hollow then they proceed to beat Trinity 12-3. In between and games and after practices Johnny is working daily with the varsity when they practice face offs. The varsity coaches notice that Johnny is beating everyone regularly. He is giving it his all in every practice as is the rest of the team. Johnny is also working on his clamps every night at home and takes 50 to 60 shots righty and lefty on the run after each practice.

CHAPTER 15:
THE HOME STRETCH

Next up for the Hawks is the Holy Family Crusaders, who the they beat in their first match up by two goals in very tough battle. This time it is a different story as the Hawks jump all over the Crusaders and win convincingly by a score of 11-4. Johnny wins 13 out of 16 face offs and Kenny has 3 goals and an assist.

The guys are feeling good going into their last game, but they realize that they can not let up. The team works hard in practice, maintains their focus and finishes every sprint at full tilt. It seems that the entire team sticks around for extra work after practice. It is a major difference from the beginning of the year when there were groans over every single sprint and the field would empty immediately after practice. No one wants the season to end.

The last game is against Riverhead and they should be a tough opponent as their JV has gone 15-4 on the season. The team is determined to come out for this one extremely aggressively. Johnny is all over the first draw and pulls it out to Jake who scoops it and gets to Nick in the box on the offensive side of the field.

The Hawks jump out to a quick 4-1 lead and wind up cruising to a 10-2 victory with all of the starters sitting out from midway through the 3rd quarter on as Coach empties the bench and plays the guys that have not gotten alot of run in the games durig the season, but have practiced hard all year long and were a big part of the team's success. The starters cheer their buddies on. It's a great way to end the season.

After the teams shake hands they head to the locker room where Coach P gathers them and tells them how proud he is of the way that they finished up the season. He tells them that if they can work like they did the last part of the season that there will be the opportunity to be a very special squad around here with big things in their future. He informs the team that there will be a list posted Monday morning on the locker room door for individual year end meetings where they will turn in equipment and uniforms. Just like that the season is abruptly over.

The JV finishes the season at 14-2. They split with Port, their fierce rival and lost to Yorktown. Johnny finished the JV year with two goals, three assists, and won an astounding 78% of his face offs. Kenny led the team with 34 goals and was second in assists with 19. His 53 points were 10 more than Nick who had 43 points. Not bad for a couple of eighth graders. All of this exceeded their expectations.

CHAPTER 16:
CALLED UP

Johnny's year end meeting with Coach P is at 2:45 on Monday. He rushes in after class ends and grabs his equipment. He walks into Coach's office and is greeted by Coach P. "Take a seat Johnny." He says, "You had a great year at the face off X. We probably won a few games this year that we would not have won had we not won as much on face offs. We were also able to open up some comfortable leads because of your work. That allowed me to play a lot of guys and get some PT (playing time) to some people that might not have gotten it otherwise. Coach Martin has noticed your work against the varsity guys and he wants you and me plus a few others to move up to Varsity for the playoff run. How about that," he says with a huge smile on his face.

Johnny is stoked. He gives Coach a big handshake and thanks him. Coach warns him that he might not get a lot of PT, but even if he just practices it should be great work for him and he will be helping the varsity push for the state championship. "Now hustle up and get ready for practice." Kenny is next up for the meeting. Johnny is sure he will be needing his equipment as well.

Johnny suits up and is about to head out the tunnel when Kenny pops out of Coach's office and says, "Yea boy, see you out there." They knuckle up and chest bump, laughing and yelling as they jump. Johnny heads out onto the field. He sees that Jake, and Vince are already out there. He can't believe it.

The whole team is fired up. They run through stretches and cals. The captains are Ryan, Danny C, the goalie and Teddy Smith (Tommy's older brother). Ryan is telling everyone that this is their shot and that he expects everyone to go all out in practices and games. He is yelling that we have two weeks left if they go all the way. He is imploring everyone to give everything that they have. The team breaks into stick work and everyone is flying through the drills. There is a lot of chatter: Here's your help! I've got backup! Break!"

CHAPTER 17:
A NEW SEASON

Coach Martin calls everyone in and says, "Gentlemen, we have a new season. We win, we move on, we lose, we go home—done for the year. We start off with the Glen Head Eagles in the county quarters. One game at a time, focus, work hard and play with your head."

Practice beings and Johnny takes notice right away that there is a jump in the speed of the game. He is focusing and going all out on everything and it is a struggle to keep up. The team runs through six on six, a riding and clearing and then coach yells for fast breaks.

Ryan heads up the line and Johnny is next. Ryan turns, fist bumps him, and says, "Good to have you up here my man."

Johnny replies, "Thanks, good to be here."

Coach blows the whistle and Ryan breaks over the midfield line and down the right alley. He fakes to the point and the defense starts to slide, he pulls his stick back and fires a rocket to lower left for a goal. Coach blows the whistle, Johnny takes off, flying down the right alley, the point defenseman starts over and Johnny moves the ball to point only to have the point dman step back and pick it off. Coach yells at Johnny that he, "must make the defensemen commit, not take two steps in his direction. DRAW THE SLIDE!" He walks up to him, puts his arm around his shoulder, and said "You just did what the defenseman wants. You let him "play you" as he points to his temple and you gave up our advantage of having an extra guy on the break. We want to draw the slide and movie it."

The team finishes up with the man up vs. man down and some sprints. Coach then tells everyone to hit the showers.

Ryan yells, "Coach, shouldn't we work on some face offs?" Coach responds, "Good idea, face off guys, Let's go."

The guys lineup on the midline and do twenty clamps and twenty rakes. They lineup with Ryan and Teddy Smith starting them off. Ryan takes it cleanly. Next up is Johnny. Johnny uses his go to quick clamp and wins the draw. Then he beats Kyle, Mike Murphy and Teddy Smith. Ryan is up again and this time he tries to chop Johnny, but Johnny is too quick, he has the ball ¾ clamped and is able to pull the ball out. Coach yells out, "Way to go freshman!"

Kenny, who is watching from the track shouts, "He's in eigth grade coach!" Coach Martin turns around and gives him a look and says, "Excuse me Mr. Brocho Cinco" as he makes quotation marks with his fingers "weren't you told to hit the showers!? You can do some sprints if you want." Kenny hits the tunnel quickly.

Coach turns around and says, "We go until someone beats Johnny."

Johnny wins eleven in a row and finally loses to Ryan who tied him up and eventually pushed him off the ball. The guys his the showers. Johnny walks home with Kenny and Ryan. Ryan tells him to keep it up at X and he might see some time in the playoffs.

Johnny pops through the door and roars to his parents that he got called up to the varsity for the playoffs. His mom, dad, and Kate rush to the door and give him a huge hug. Everyone is so happy for him except for Kim, who is distraught and disgusted. She makes a face and says, "This is ridiculous. Out of hand. Why did they call HIM up? Mr. Two Goals All Year."

It cracks up Johnny's parents that Kim is embarrassed that Johnny is doing so well and is invading her "turf" and her group of friends.

Johnny pounds down his dinner and has to get to work on the books because he has a Science test and an English test this week. He has to keep his mind from drifting to lacrosse and he studies until he knows the material pretty well. He has two more days to study for science and three more for English. He does fifty quick clamps, twenty-five chops and twenty-five rakes. He tries to get to sleep, but lies in bed for at least two hours with his mind racing.

Johnny enters seventh period for his Science exam. He feels good because he is prepared. The exam is tough but Johnny feels as if he has done well. Everyone else seems to be complaining about the test being "unfair" or "too hard." Johnny just nods and smiles as he knows that he did well on it. He starts getting butterflies as eighth period begins and is starting to get nervous and anxious as he enters the locker room.

Smitty has the tunes blasting and everyone is glaring eyes as they suit up. People are banging lockers and shouting encouragement to each other.

CHAPTER 18:
GLEN HEAD

Coach calls everyone in and the music gets shut off. There is silence in the room as Jack Martin is loved, respected and held in awe by all players. His voice is hoarse from years of yelling from the sidelines. He goes over situations, substitutions and lineups. He finishes up with "Hustle, defend, clear, GROUNDBALLS and attack the goal. If we do this the game is ours. Two lines behind Ryan and Smitty out the tunnel and into warm-ups."

The teams lineup for the face off. Ryan is taking the first one and wins it easily. The Hawks move it around the outside, but quickly turn it over. The Glen Head Eagles are able to clear and settle on offense, they work it behind and run a two man pick and roll behind the goal. The attack man with the ball draws a double and is able to hit the roll man who streaks to fire a one-on-one. Luckily he fails to get a good angle and is stuffed by a Dan. He is able to hit Ryan on the breakout who has a step on his man and pulls away from him. It is a classic four on three with Ryan hitting the point, it then goes down low and across the cage to Vince, who buries it. 1-0 good guys.

Ryan wins the next face and jets down the right alley. He fires a high bouncer into the upper left corner. This sets the tone and makes the rest of the team more settled and confident. The team hustles, defends and pushes it into the offensive zone. They take a 5-1 halftime lead and are leading 8-1 to begin the fourth. Coach tells Johnny to take the face. He bolts out to the X. There are shouts from the sideline and the stands, "Your ball Johnny," "Let's go, keep the momentum going Johnny."

Johnny wins it cleanly on a clamp and pulls it to the side. He scoops it and sprints to the box, dumps it to an attack man and is on the bench in what seems like a total of five seconds. Jake gives him knuckles and says, "Nice bro, NIIIIICE!" nodding his head and banging on Johnny's shoulder. Johnny wins three more face offs to go four for four on the day. After the last one, Jake yells out, "My boy is automatic! Freakin' automatic!" the Hawks cruise to a 10-3 victory.

The locker room is jubilant when coach Martin walks in and says, "Gentlemen, nice effort today, but get ready to work. This is just the first step and it gets a whole lot tougher from here on out. If we work hard and make sacrifices we can do great things. Westport beat Westbury today so we will play them on Saturday. If anyone needs to see the trainer, get in there. Nice job tonight. Get some rest."

Johnny meets his dad outside the school locker room and they walk home together. They are pretty quiet, but Johnny's father tells him how proud he is of him. He is proud, because he knows how hard his son has worked and how much he has prepared. He loves his son and is happy to see his hard work payoff. He can't believe how quickly things are happening.

CHAPTER 19: WESTPORT

Coach is right about the Westport game being a lot tougher. The Wolf Pack jump out to a 4-2 first quarter lead. They have a lightning quick middie that gets his hands free and fires bullets and they also have an attackman that has hit cutters for three assists in the first quarter.

The second quarter begins with a Wolf Pack possession. The defense gets a stop, but Westport rides like the Wolf Pack. They cause a turnover and score an easy one in transition. The Wolf Pack win the next face off and score on a fast break 6-2 and Coach Martin is incensed. He calls a time out. He barks that, "Westport has out hustled us and beaten us to every single groundball. We are getting caught ball watching on defense. Who is going to step-up. Anyone want to go home for the season? I don't! Bring it in! We're going with Price on the face off. Harris and Ryan on the wings. Be the best on three. 1-2-3 BE THE BEST!"

"Let's go Johnny!" "C'mon Johnny!"

Johnny bounces out to face off. He focuses and gets set. He explodes on the whistle and pulls it to

Ryan for an easy groundball The Hawks work it around and get it to Ryan up top, he split dodges left to right and down the right alley. The defender tries to push him hard down the side and the slide comes early but Ryan sees it and rolls back to the inside he takes two steps, jumps and fires a bounce shot off the far pipe and in. 6-3. Johnny wins the next draw and the teams exchange possessions until Sean Stevens cuts off a pick and receives a feed from behind from Jack Mac for a quick stick to lower left with twenty-two seconds left in the half. Johnny trots out to X, readies himself and focuses on the whistle. At the first peep of the whistle he explodes into the clamp and is able to go forward with it. Johnny breaks for the ball but sees that Ryan has a line on the ball and two steps on the defending wingman. Johnny boxes out the Wolf Pack face off man as Ryan sweeps in. Johnny turns and sprints to the box and is almost off the field when he hears the crowd roar. He turns to see the players on the field mobbing Ryan. 6-5 with thirteen seconds on the clock. Coach grabs Johnny by the arm and tells him to try to rake it forward for a break.

Johnny rakes but misses. His momentum is all going forward. Johnny can only look over his shoulder and watch as the face off man from the Wolf Pack sprints downfield with the ball.

Luckily Jake is playing the defensive wing and gets a good jump on the whistle. He takes an angle and forces the Westport FOGO (Face off and get off) to his left hand with a slap, gets into his body and shoves him down the side and follows with a hard slap to the gloves as the opposing middie releases an off balance shot that sails off course and out of bounds as the half expires.

Johnny jogs off with Jake and says, "Thanks for havin my back, bro."

Jake replies, " No problem, my man. You win the draws and I'll get the D end."

The guys gather in the locker room as coach begins to make his adjustments. They are going to go to a zone on defense and look to work some mumbo sets on offense as the Wolf Pack have started to slide to double team Ryan very quickly.

Johnny wins the first draw of the half going forward off a quick clamp. He leads a classic fast break by drawing the slide hitting the point where it goes down low and over to Sean on the left. He dips and dunks for a goal, but is decked from behind on a blatantly late hit. The ref throws the flag as the crowd screams in outrage. Sean doesn't get up. The coach and trainer run out. They tell him to stay down. Sean finally is helped to his feet after several minutes. There are shouts of "Great goal Sean!" "Way to go kid, way to be tough!" and "You da man Sean!"

Coach Martin tells Kenny to fill in for Sean on the man up. The team gets set for the man up face. When the ref blows the whistle, Johnny pounces on it with a clamp, he rotates over the ball and pops the ball over the midline. It is an easy groundball for Ryan as the wing cannot go over midfield as they would be offsides due to the penalty.

The Hawks go with a classic 3-3 set. After about forty seconds of working the ball, Kenny breaks off and circles behind the ball as the team rotates the ball from the lefty wing up top with everyone moving the ball and rotating on a cut to the ball as it circles around the outside . It leaves a two on one with Vince and Kenny. Vince hits Kenny circling around the crease. Kenny buries it in the upper right corner! Little Shane McInnis leads the student section in chanting, "Brocho Cinco! Broch Cinco!".

Johnny wins the remaining possessions and the team scores six unanswered goals before Westport finally cracks the Hawk's zone defense to make the score 11-7 which is how the game would end.

The locker room is boisterous with the squad yelling , hooting and laughing. Tunes are cranking.

Coach pulls the team together. He starts with "Gentlemen we played well in the second half today and WE GET TO MOVE ON!" The team erupts with shouts and applause. Coach puts up his hands to quiet everyone and waits for silence before he says, "However, if we play on Thursday the way we played in the first half today we will not be moving on after Port. Let's get it together. We have two days of practice. Let's make them count and get after it. Some of the guys have never played at Hofstra. That field is the same size as ours. We WILL

WIN there the same way that we win here—defense, groundballs, and pushing it up the field.

As Johnny passes Coach's office on the way out, he gets called in by the coach! He tells Johnny to take a seat and says, "I didn't know what to expect when we brought you up on the varsity. I really thought that you would just help in practice, MAYBE get some mop up duty if we had a seven or eight goal lead, but I am glad that you are here. We might not be playing on Thursday for the Long Island Championship without you. You were great today, but you will only play if Ryan is losing the face offs. If he can win, you have to understand that I want the ball in the stick of a two time All American, right?" Johnny nods his head. Then the coach says, "Be ready though because Ryan had a tough time with Ainge the last time that we played them. I want you to watch the film of the face offs with Ryan and prepare. Face offs will be key!" He then tosses him a ball, it has the date and score of the game and says Johnny Price nine of ten FOs. Coach then says, "That belongs to you. Great job."

CHAPTER 20:
LONG ISLAND CHAMPIONSHIP

There is an air of determination in practice as the team gets ready for the Long Island Championship vs. their hated rivals from Port Jefferson. The coach keeps practice moving and the guys are crisp. They hustle through warm-ups and have an intense scrimmage! The faceoff guys stay after practice and really get after each other. Everyone is fired up for the game and they know that they have a serious challenge at the face off X against Kevin Ainge, who has committed to Drexel as a FOGO. The guys hit the showers and Ryan grabs the films of Port's last several games. Johnny and Ryan head home. They decide to go home for dinner, bang out their homework and Ryan will head over to Johnny's around 9:30 to watch film.

Johnny grabs dinner with his parents and sisters. His father and mother are asking about practice and the upcoming Port game. His mom has made a terrific sauce with sausage, pork and meatballs. It is served over penne and is a family favorite. Kim is talking about the prom on Saturday. She gets upset whenever the subject changes from the prom, her dress, or how she is going to wear her hair. She starts in on her mom and dad as soon as they ask anything about lacrosse. Johnny gives her a look and says, "You better run upstairs and get all dolled up, cause Ryan is coming over at 9:30." Everyone turns to look at the clock, when they look back, Kim's seat is empty. The rest of the family smiles and let's out a laugh.

When Ryan arrives the whole family greets him. Kim changed her outfit four times, did her makeup and blew our her hair.

The guys head downstairs to watch film. The clip shows about sixty of Ainge's face offs. It is very impressive. He had a quick clamp, usually wins it so cleanly that he can pop the ball forward. The guys practice quick clamps in the basement. They do about one hundred each. The guys go upstairs and sit down to watch TV. Ryan asks Kim if she has a second and they step into the foyer. Johnny wonders what's up. Ryan returns and watches TV and Kim comes in to join them which surprises Johnny. Kim is texting her friends and her phone is constantly buzzing as she is getting numerous texts back from them. Ryan eventually heads home and Kim blurts out that Ryan has asked her to the prom. She is hugging her mom and jumping around. She leaves to talk to and text all of her friends.

The team enters the field to begin stretching. They line up in seven rows with the captains up front facing them. Port is already on the field and into their stick drills. The crowd is pouring into the stadium.

The team has been salivating to get their revenge from their regular season loss. They want to beat their rival so badly that the players agree that this game means more to them than a state championship. The team's intensity only builds through warm-ups. Everyone lines up on the sidelines for the Star Spangled Banner when the players remove their helmets it is evident that they are sweating already. Everyone looks to the flag singing the national anthem. Johnny notices his leg shaking and pumping uncontrollably. The crowd roars in approval as the student singer completes the anthem. Coach says "Everyone in. Gentlemen, we all know that this is the Long Island Championship against Port like we hoped it would be at the beginning of the year. They got us during the season, but this is the one that counts, the ONE THAT WE WILL REMEMBER. DEFENSE, GROUNDBALLS, PUSH IT! Now let's go out and TAKE IT! 1-2-3" The team screams: BE THE BEST!

The teams line up for the ref's instructions. Johnny surveys the crowd and guesses that there are four or five thousand people and they are still coming in.

Ainge controls the opening face off and Port Jefferson settles into their first possession. They take it behind to play a little two man game at X. Smitty jumps off his man to pick up the ball on a switch. The Port attack man realizes the on ball defender doesn't switch so he rolls away from the double and hits the picking attackman who has released and is streaking to the goal. Dano hugs the pipe and stands tall. The attack fakes high. Dano stands his ground and as the attacker reaches around him to shoot low, Dano drives his stick to the ground and stuffs him one-on-one. The crowd and the Hawk's bench go crazy. Teddy Smith scoops the loose ball and flips it to Dan. Dan hits Ryan on an outlet. The Hawks push it and have a slow five on four break. Ryan pops it over to Jake who two hops and looks ready to fire a rocket with the long pole but snaps a pass at the last second to Kenny down low. Kenny grabs the ball and Mr. Automatic fakes to the lefty goalie's stick side only to bury it off hip on the rear side. The crowd explodes. Hawks 1-0. The "Brocho Cinco" chant is getting louder with more people joining with every goal that Kenny scores. His parents are totally dumbfounded. The whole scene is pretty funny. Ainge wins the draw forward and fakes to the point on the break steps in and lets an overhand laser go. Dano gets a piece of the ball on the off stick side but the ball deflects into the net: 1 all. Ainge then wins the next draw and takes it to the hoop. He is drilled by Smitty, but the ref throws a flag. Port goes 3-3 formation and the Hawks counter with the middle man playing a string and sliding and sluffing in from the top center man to the crease attack man. Port moves the ball well and as the center middie steps in the string pops in and the lower defender pinch to the crease. Port continues to move it until the top center middies finds a seam and fires the ball lower right to the lefty attackman on the door step. He quick sticks it in top right. Dano had no shot. 2-1 bad guys. The quarter ends at 2-1. In between periods it is announced over the PA system that 84 college coaches have checked in with the press box.

The teams pick up the intensity in the second quarter as the two sides settle in offensively. The Port lefty is making alot of saves but the Hawks are starting to get to him. On the other end, Dano was making spectacular saves left and right. Two of the saves were point blank. He kept the Hawks in the game while under pressure the entire first half. The half ends 8-5 Port.

At halftime the Coach goes over adjustments. One of the first, is that we need possessions—Boys they are beating us to the ball. Johnny you are going to take the first face in the second half. BOYS WE NEED THE BALL, our shots are starting to go in WE NEED TO KEEP FIRING. WE NEED TO POSSESS THE BALL. It's very simple. They can't score if we have the ball! LET'S GET IN GENTS! They think that they are moving on! They think that WE ARE GOING HOME! NOW WHAT'S IT GOING TO BE?"

Ryan huddles the guys and says, "Look everyone needs to go all out every play. WE HAVE WORKED TOO HARD TO GO HOME NOW. THAT'S NOT HAPPENING! EVERYONE IN TIGHT 1-2-3- BE THE BEST!"

Johnny goes out for the face with Ryan and Jake on the wings. The crowd roars. Johnny hears his teammates shout encouragement. Ainge cocks his head and says, "Oh look, a new punk. It's going to be a long day kid."

Johnny focuses. They get ready. The ref says, "Down" then he whistles. Johnny explodes into his clamp. He is surprised that he is a fair amount quicker than Ainge. He cleanly pulls the ball out to Ryan. He jogs off to cheers from the crowd. The Hawks spin it once and it winds up with Ryan up top 1-4 formation. He drives a split dodge right to left. The slide comes quickly. Kenny pops out and receives a feed from Ryan. As he turns and fires, he is laid out by the second side. The ball ricochets off the pipe and is scooped and cleared by a Port middie. The crushing hit leaves Kenny woozy but he is able to shake it off.

Port possesses the ball for a solid three minutes firing on goal. Dano repeatedly deflects and turns away shots. Many go wide and are backed up by the Port attack. They finally put one home for a 9-5 lead.

Johnny hurries out for the face. He takes it cleanly again.

This time he takes it himself and dishes it off to Vince before he heads off. Jack settles it behind goal. He drives hard left, rolls back right at X and fires a no look feed to Vince on the crease. Vince buries it off hip and the HAWKS get some life back. The HAWKS score two more quick one comes off of a fast break on the face where Johnny hits the point, Aidan moves it down to Kenny who lets one go low to high and snags the upper corner. The other goal came off a ride where Kenny and Vince caused a turnover and fed a streaking Aidan who dodges the goalie about five yards above the crease and Fires into an empty net. The score is 9-8 and the crowd is going wild.

Johnny is able to win the next draw and go forward with it. The defenseman baits Johnny by faking the slide. Johnny passes to point. Just as Johnny lets the ball go the defender steps in the passing lane, picks off the pass and takes off. Everyone's momentum has taken them moving into the HAWKS offensive end and the big defender is able to blow by the middies. He gets to about twelve yards and fires an overhead rocket upper left. The ball hits the pipe and goes in as Dan has a tough time getting a read on the ball coming off the long pole's stick. The quarter ends 10-8 Port.

The boys bring it in. There are shouts of "EVERY-THING WE'VE GOT!" "FIFTEEN MINUTES, ALL OUT!" "GOT TO HAVE IT" and "FOURTH QUARTER'S ALL OURS!"

Johnny pulls out the face off to it to Ryan. Ryan inverts and takes the ball behind. He dodges like a man possessed and beats his man to the left side on a split dodge. Ryan reaches goal line extended and causes the slide to hesitate with a fake pass to the crease. The hesitation is all that he needs. He takes two steps around the goal and beats the lefty goalie over his right shoulder.

Johnny wins the next draw and has won all seven face offs that he has taken. Vince just misses on a shot but the HAWKS retain possession and put four more on goal. Unfortunately the big lefty saves them all. Port clears and they settle the ball. They are taking time off the clock. They methodically work the ball around the perimeter and take over two minutes off the clock until

Smitty catches his attack man with a poke check just as he receives the ball. A wild battle for the ball takes place and finally Cade Quinn burst from the pile with the ball. He takes off screaming "Middie back" at the top of his lungs. He brings the ball into the offensive end and looks to the point. He draws the slide, hits Aidan who fires across low to Vince for a one-on-one dip and dunk. 10 all as the crowd explodes.

Port coach screams, "DO NOT SLIDE TO LONG POLES OR EIGHTH GRADERS DAMMIT!"

On the following face off Ainge changes his technique. He chops over the ball and catches Johnny off guard. He is able to pull the ball to the side and forward. Ainge scoops it for a fast break. Port takes advantage and just like that, Port has the lead again 11-10 Port with 3:08 left on the clock.

Johnny is ready for the chop move on the next face off and is able to fight off Ainge and eventually pull it out towards Ryan, but he doesn't get alot of momentum on the draw and the Port long pole steps between Johnny and Ryan and scoops the ball. Port puts the ball behind the net and gets their offensive players on the field. With 1:40 left on the clock Coach calls for Dano to come out and double the ball. The attack man drives at Smitty, fakes left and dodges right. He is able to split Smitty and Dano. He outraces them to the goal and Port goes up 12-10 with 1:14 left on the clock.

Ainge goes back to clamping on the ensuing face off. Johnny wins it cleanly. The Hawks push it behind and Aidan Quinn posts up his man on the right side. He draws a double from the wing. Aidan dumps it to Kenny who has stepped in and has a good look. His shot skips off the crossbar and out of bounds. Vince has backed it up fifty-two seconds left. They work the ball up top to Ryan. He split dodges to his left, jumps and fires the ball just off target. Hawks ball behind the net with thirty-nine seconds to go.

Coach calls time out. He calls for a 1-4-1 with Ryan up top. He says "Ryan they are going to slide to you quickly. I want the wing to cut through and we will pick and run a Mumbo cut underneath. We'll get this score and get a time out so we can set up the tying goal. 1-2-3 "BE THE BEST!"

The ball gets worked up top to Ryan, he starts his dodge and Port switches to zone. Ryan beats his man by a step but is getting pushed down the side and here comes the slide. Ryan rolls back left, takes two steps and hits Kenny who has popped off of a pick on the crease. Kenny catches the ball, turns, gets a good look and fires. The ball hits the twine and the announcer screams over the loudspeaker that, "Brocho Cinco has just made it a 1 goal game!" At least 2500 people Scream "Brocho Cinco" " BrochO CincO" with Shane McInnis leading the way.

Coach Martin tells the guys to "push if we get the opportunity, otherwise to get it to Ryan behind on an invert with cutters in front. Ryan take it to the rack, draw and dump or finish it yourself." As they break the huddle Ryan knuckles Johnny and says, "Our ball, bro! If you get the break they might not slide to you. Don't hit the goalie—it goes in or we back it up, but don't hit the goalie."

The face off men get ready and Johnny notices the change in Ainge's stance—he is going to chop and try to tie him up. The whistle blows, Ainge chops, Johnny drops the head of his stick backwards and pushes the ball forward—right under Ainge's stick. The ball pops forward and Johnny sprints after it. He scoops it in full stride. He looks to the point and shoulder fakes as if to pass, the slide does not come, he continues down the alley looking for the lower attack man. The defenders have locked on Johnny continues to about eight or nine yards, steps and lets one go aiming four inches inside the left pipe. The slide finally comes, and Johnny gets wrecked. He doesn't see or hear anything for a second or so. Then he realizes that the crowd is roaring. He looks and sees the ball in the net. All tied up with 4 seconds left on the clock.

There is a shooting pain in Johnny's right shoulder. All of the fingers in his left hand are numb. He tries to get up but he stumbles. Coach calls his last timeout for regulation. He decides that Johnny cannot go. He is putting Ryan out there for the last face off. The Hawks are MAN UP due to the cross check call on the late hit on Johnny. He instructs the team to hold the ball if they do they will retain possession for overtime because of the penalty.

Ainge wins the draw but Ryan chases him to the

ball and checks it away from him. The period ends without possession and the teams huddle before overtime is to begin. Coach asks, "Johnny can you face off?" Everyone looks at Johnny and he replies, "I've got it coach." The players all slap his helmet and yell "yeah man, your ball kid!"

Johnny walks out to the face off X. His shoulder is killing him. The players get set. On the whistle Johnny clamps, Ainge smashes into Johnny's injured right shoulder and pain rips through him. He rotates ¾ around to his left and feebly rakes it to Jake in the offensive zone. Port has moved an attack man to the wing but he cannot go over the midfield line due to the penalty. Coach calls time out as soon as Jake scoops it. Joe, the trainer runs to Jake and helps him to the bench. Joe gently removes his jersey and his shoulder pads. They tape ice to the shoulder with an ace bandage. Joe says to him, "Kid you probably just won the championship for us." The teams break their huddles. The teams start in a 3-3. Ryan rips a shot just wide to the near side. They set it up again and run the sneak two-on-one, Ryan fakes down to Kenny. He steps in and lets it fly over the goalie's left shoulder for the Long Island Championship.

It was Ryan's sixth goal of the night. He wasn't going to be denied. The team piles on top of him and the crowd goes insane. The players line up and shake hands then the celebration starts all over again.

The team is gathered around as Ryan is interviewed

after the game. The reporters asked "How it felt to bury the game winner in the Long Island Championship in overtime?"

Ryan responds, "It was great, but we wouldn't have had the chance if it weren't for Danny in the net, tough defense all game by Smitty and the boys, and how about Johnny Price, the 8th grader, winning the face offs and his game tying goal That was MINT! The team breaks into a roar with shouts of Yea Jonny! Johnny kid!

CHAPTER 21:
PROM PARTY

Kim is hosting the pre prom party for about twenty prom couples.

The weather is great and everyone chills on the patio out back. All the guys are sporting their tuxes and having a good time. Johnny is hanging out in his flip flops, shorts, shoulder sling and a t-shirt. Teddy Smith walks over and high fives him. He throws his arm over Johnny's shoulder and Johnny grimaces in pain as Teddy tells the crowd, "This is the guy that won the Hawks the Long Island Championship!" Let's hear it for Johnny! Everyone whoops it up.

Kim turns to her mom with a look of distain and says, "This is my prom party and it's all about him! Ryan barely even knows I'm here!"

When it's time to take the group shot, Ryan tells Johnny to jump in. Kim just rolls her eyes and shakes her head.

Smitty keeps popping in and out of one of the limos and as the party ends and everyone gets in the car to go, Johnny sees that Teddy's limo has beers realizes that is why he kept going in the car.

The cars are set to pull out, and Carl and Janet wave and tell them to "Have fun, be safe."

Smitty got drunk that night and threw up all over the limo. This ruined the night for all four couples in the car. He also proceeded to throw up half the night. Coach Martin booted him off the team as soon as he heard. Teddy's father tried pleading with Coach, but there was no changing Jack Martin's mind. Teddy knew the rules and chose not to follow them.

CHAPTER 21:
STATE SEMI FINALS VS.
YORKTOWN

Teddy being suspended would prove to be devastating as Yorktown's top attack man, Rob Porter would have six goals in the semis. Teddy was supposed to have guarded him. Ryan played well and scored four goals, but had a tough time at the X. He was up against Johnny's buddy, Riggs from the beginning of the year. He had moved up to varsity around mid season. Riggs had two goals and was twelve for fifteen on face offs. The Hawks could not muster much offense besides Ryan's four goals and wound up losing 11-6. The season went from sky high to a crashing thud.

Johnny told his dad how miserable he felt watching from the sidelines and unable to help. He also told him how he felt so horribly for Ryan, with his high school lacrosse suddenly over.

Ken replied, "Ryan has much bigger games ahead in his future at UVA and he had a high school career that any kid would dream of. You my friend have four more chances and alot of work to do."

Johnny just nodded his head and said, "Definitely have alot of work to do.